THE HAUNTED QUILL

An Anthology

of

Historical Speculative Fiction

NEW YORK
MEGARA PUBLISHING

MEGARA
PUBLISHING

Megara Publishing Inc.
447 Broadway
New York, NY 10013
megarapublishing.com

This is a work of fiction. Names, characters, organizations, places, events, and incidents are either products of the author's imagination or are used fictitiously. Any resemblance to actual persons, living or dead, or actual events is purely coincidental.

Title: The Haunted Quill
Authors: Jordan Taylor, Laura Hennessey DeSena, LH Moore, Stephen K. Pettersson, Henry Herz, Jane Nightshade, Colleen Ennen, Caren Gussoff Sumption.
Editor: Kate Francia
Copyeditor: Mira Singer
Illustrators: Kate Francia & Mira Singer
ISBN: 978-1-7373477-2-9

Manufactured in the United States of America

TABLE OF CONTENTS

La Orpheline

Jordan Taylor

Act I: The Kingdom of the Broken Fan

T his story begins at the end. The orphan is found by her new family *adoptif.*

Look: she is here, asleep in a row of plush seats in the Grande Salle, her bare brown feet tucked under the tattered hem of her skirts. Above her soars the painted ceiling and the many chandeliers of the Opéra le Peletier, which is, in the brief time of this story, the national opera of France. Around her stand the members of the production company – the angular Costume Mistress, the rotund Directeur de Théâtre, the seamstresses and the members of the orchestra and the many brawny stagehands – all peering at her intently and holding their breath, as if she is a princess in a tale. There is some debate about turning her out into the streets – for in the time of this story, an extra mouth to feed in Paris could mean hunger for all.

Look: she awakes. She sits up and blinks at the company with her great dark eyes, saying nothing, unafraid of the many faces surrounding her. She is dark, for a Parisian, with slim tawny limbs and thick brown hair that falls around her thin shoulders. There is dust and grime and dirt on her face.

The Head Soprano sails into the scene in full crinolines, late for her rehearsal, and elbows her way to the front of the crowd. When she sees the silent child, she twitters, discomfited, "We can always eat *her*, if she doesn't work out," and flutters her fan at her face.

So the child stays.

She becomes a kind of assistant to the Costume Mistress and the other, more experienced seamstresses – her nimble fingers, as she helps piece together the sopranos' elaborate gowns, sewing stitches so fine they can scarcely be seen.

During the opera's productions she climbs about in the wooden and paste-board town of backstage like a lithe little cat, peeping out at the audience from a perch in the rafters, her face alight with that circle of chandeliers that hangs like a glittering universe from the domed ceiling.

At night, she makes her bed amongst the tombstones on top of the rolling platform of a graveyard set-piece once used in the production of *Don Giovanni*.

They call her la Orpheline.

* * *

The scene: the little costuming room in the warren of backstage, three years after la Orpheline's mysterious arrival at the Opéra le Peletier. The Head Soprano stands in front center position, pinned into the gown for her upcoming role as the Countess in *The Marriage of Figaro*.

La Orpheline and a group of her fellow seamstresses kneel around her as they work on the gown. The room is entirely taken up by its long train. Bolts of silk and taffeta and chiffon, fake jewels and ostrich feathers, tumble from an open closet at the back of the room, as if the characters inhabit a shabby wooden Aladdin's cave. The Soprano is speaking, as she often does, of her new benefactor, who has promised to be in the most expensive box in the theater on opening night.

"He is not handsome," the Soprano admits. "But he is something else. *Magnetic*." She raises her clear blue eyes and white arms towards the low wooden ceiling, as if on stage. "And terribly rich!"

The pinned gown shifts around her as she moves, the black silk rustling. It's high-necked, the skirt covered in tragic black rosettes, severe and beautiful against the Soprano's pale hair and skin. The role of the Countess is that of an aggrieved wife, in competition with her own maid for the attentions of the Count.

The Soprano is no longer as young as she once was.

The Soprano cries out and smacks la Orpheline across the face with her fan as she is pricked by the gown's loose pins, the delicate silk ripping at her waist, the fan's wooden skeleton cracking against the sharp bones of la Orpheline's cheek.

"You clumsy little slut! Now you've ruined my fan as well!"

La Orpeline puts her hand to her face, stung.

"But he has another woman," the Soprano continues as if nothing has happened. La Orpheline and her fellow seamstresses begin unpinning the gown, the silk drifting to the floor in dark waves around the Soprano's legs. "The one woman," the Soprano turns away from their lowered faces, gazing dramatically and a tad wistfully into the middle distance, "for whom even I may be no match."

* * *

The Marriage of Figaro. Opening night. Silk and jewels wink in the light of the chandeliers as the crowd passes in and out of their boxes and peers unashamedly at their neighbors through raised opera glasses. The red velvet and mahogany wood of the plush seats glow under the brilliant house lights.

The velvet stage curtains are closed for the brief intermission between the first two acts.

Look up, at the gilded carvings from which they hang. Look: do you see that little brown face?

La Orpheline gazes down at the crowd, her bare legs wrapped tightly around a wooden beam in the backstage scaffolding, her arms resting on the gilded carvings. She can smell the varnish used on the wood, talcum, a dozen different perfumes. At such a distance she would, to anyone else, seem to be nothing but another carving– a cherub, perhaps, or more likely a lovely sort of demon.

At least to anyone but the inhabitants of the nearest box, the one in which the Soprano's benefactor has promised to appear.

It has been empty through the entire first act.

But look – someone is entering that box now, just in time for the Soprano's first solo.

A tall, thin man in impeccable black tails, a silk top hat tucked under one arm, is backing into the alcove, his face turned away from la Orpheline. He extends a white hand to help someone into the box behind him, and a woman steps into view.

La Orpheline's breath catches in her throat.

The woman has a perfect heart-shaped face and enormous eyes of a deep blue that in the light of the chandeliers is almost violet. She wears a black velvet gown cut shockingly low, the antithesis of the Soprano's own, her chestnut curls resting in her *décolletage*. A priceless collar of diamonds circles her white neck, producing a blinding flash that must be seen across the theater as she emerges into the light.

La Orpheline has never seen her before, and yet she knows her at once.

She is Paris's most famous courtesan, the one they call la Reine des Fées, and gossip about in voices hushed with awe. She is said to be so beautiful that all the kings of Europe wish to have her, and that – more shocking still – she has turned them all down, one by one.

As she looks at her now, la Orpheline can almost believe it.

La Reine des Fées folds her hands demurely and sinks into her seat, as if unaware of the staring crowd, her gown pooling around her like ink.

The benefactor turns, one hand on the small of her back as he joins her, and for the first time in three years la Orpheline sees his face.

A tremor comes over la Orpheline's body, her legs shaking where they grip the beam, her torso swaying as she fights to keep her balance.

She gasped audibly as he turned, and now he looks up, like a hound sighting a scent, his cold eyes narrowing and then widening as he catches sight of la Orpheline's face. La Reine des Fées follows his eyes, her coral lips open in surprise.

La Orpheline's heart pounds once, twice, three times. She hears the snap of a wire cage closing, feels the prick of the bone knife twisting beneath her trembling ribcage, the horrible agony as her catskin is peeled back, forcing the change.

The house lights go down.

She never imagined what he might have done with the power he stole from her, how different his circumstances might have become in three years.

The stage lights come up.

The curtains open.

The Soprano steps onto the stage beneath this frozen tableau, her arms spread wide, her long train moving across the floor like water. Applause ripples through the crowd. The Soprano looks up to the box where her benefactor has promised to be, and her face freezes into a mask when she sees who accompanies him.

La Orpheline watches the Soprano's eyes dart from side to side, taking in her benefactor's shocked face and upturned eyes, and then the Soprano turns her own head, so slowly, so slightly, that it might be only the continuation of her opening pose. Her eyes climb up, up to la Orpheline's own. Fury twists her features.

La Orpheline's hands, sweating now in fright, slip from the carved arch, and she falls.

* * *

Act II: The Republic of the Broken Leg

A flashback to a miserable set of rooms on the Rue de la Lune, in the Temple district near la Place du Papier. The wooden and stone floors are carpeted in a thick layer of dust. The damp kitchen is covered in mold and ooze and unspeakable grime. The furniture is fine but sparse and from another century.

This lateral maze of rooms makes up the back half of a crumbling row home with few windows. By night, the neighbors can hear strange voices and inhuman shrieks through the walls, can smell blood and sulfur creeping through the cracks in the stones.

They are too afraid to complain. The rooms are home to a magician, and who knows what arcane arts he may have at his disposal, perfect for ferreting out neighbors with loose tongues?

And besides, in a time when it is never certain who holds the city, and for whom, to whom does one complain?

Each morning, the Magician emerges into the sun, dressed in the same well-made, perfectly pressed black suit and tall silk top hat, which shadows his piercing dark eyes and the white knife of his face.

The Rue de la Lune is a hidden twist in a snarl of cobblestone streets covered in the stalls of booksellers – a world of wood, stone, canvas, and paper where dappled cats slink through the shadows and bask in the sun. By day, the Magician peruses the stalls of the booksellers or sits in the shabby café in la Place de Papier, where he watches the secretive cats and the bands of roving child thieves who pick the scholars' pockets.

There is one cat and one child who the Magician watches more than all the others.

She is a girl child, a thief with tiny nimble fingers, and a small cat, dappled brown and black with a little swirl of white above its pink nose, as if marked there by an artist's brush. They have the same liquid dark eyes.

By day he sips at his weak greasy tea and thinks of how to take her, his long fingers with their bitten nails tapping against the dirty porcelain of the cup.

By night he constructs the tools he will need – a cage of glinting wires whose little door springs closed with a touch, a wicked knife with a bone blade over which he speaks a litany of forgotten spells from one of his books.

And he waits.

* * *

La Orpheline hobbles around backstage on a set of little wooden crutches from le Peletier's prop department, swinging her broken leg. See her now, raising her pointed chin to gaze wistfully into the rafters, her little hand brushing her hair out of her face? For the remainder of the run of *The Marriage of Figaro* she is confined to the ground, and the Costume Mistress tells her she is lucky to be alive, lucky that the tenor playing Figaro was there to help break her fall.

She may never climb again.

She stays out of the Soprano's way as much as possible, slipping away whenever the Soprano needs help with her costume. By day she sews mechanically through the performances, thinking of nothing but where she could go to hide from the Magician, of what she could become, her broken leg dragging behind her like an animal with its foot caught in a trap.

At night, her head rests beneath the fake plaster of a little marble tombstone like a headboard to her bed – *Repose en paix* – and she dreams of her catskin.

She dreams of the night wind in her whiskers and the moon in her eyes, of the balance that comes with her tail, the freedom of three good legs, until the face of the Magician swims into her dreams, his white hands reaching for her like the hands of a skeleton clawing up from its grave.

* * *

She fights him, at first.

Close your eyes if you must.

We're in those miserable rooms again.

She fights him with the kind of ferocity that the Magician should have expected from a little stray cat. But there is no escape from his maze of rooms, he made sure of this – spells and guards placed on even the smallest possible exits. Eventually, hungry and exhausted – No! – she is giving in.

The Magician has hidden the catskin – hidden it somewhere, he claims, it will never be found, no matter how she searches.

And she does search.

When he goes out by day, she looks; she opens dust-filled drawers and cupboards, claws beneath dirty floorboards and behind bricks, peers behind greasy pictures and furniture and mirrors, but no, no, it is not there.

He brings it out from its hiding place only when he wishes for her to teach him.

"Show me how it works."

And she helps him squeeze in, his longer bones buckling and then showing through in odd places when he's completed the change. Wearing her skin.

Sometimes she retches.

Sometimes he does.

And then he disappears into the Paris night, leaving her alone with the stub of a candle and the shrieks of his servants and the whispering of his books.

And no catskin.

Every time he uses the skin he becomes a little more powerful, a little wealthier, his spells and his alchemy working a little too well. And yet the change – so much worse for him – takes a toll on his body, so that he soon learns he must use it only sparingly.

But for all that he learns, there are still things about which he is apparently ignorant, and so he returns home one morning, shrugging the catskin off in his damp front hall, to find that she has escaped.

He must not have noticed that while he was learning from her, she was also learning from him.

He must not know that sometimes a girl's will to survive is strong enough she is willing to leave a piece of herself behind.

* * *

Act III: The Empire of Broken Hearts

The curtain opens on a scene from la Maison des Rêves, on the Rue de Louis, and a very different girl. Look at her raise her arms as she sings in the velvet parlor, the rapture on her exquisite young face! What you can't see: her heart, full to the brim with yearning, and the cracks on its surface which have already begun to form.

La Maison des Rêves is a jewel box of a house, fake bedroom after fake bedroom of silks and satins opening onto a curved balcony over which men in evening wear hang to look down upon the salon. The Madame of the house accompanies the girl on the piano while the other women laugh and pretend to toss back drinks with their suitors.

The girl considers the bedrooms fake for no one sleeps there, the women instead sharing simple dormitories on the uppermost floor. She shares these dormitories as well, and calls the Madame "Madame," despite the fact that the Madame is her mother.

If the house is a jewel box, then the girls are its jewels – closely guarded, and priceless, at least until the markets fall and they are worth nothing more than a loaf of bread. The Madam, its owner, keeps the jewels crushed tightly in her hungry fist.

This girl, perhaps she is not so different from the other after all.

If this girl is to be a jewel, then she will at least be a jewel taken from the box, one which can be seen and admired by all. So she uses a few of her precious coins to buy herself a book of voice exercises, and she flatters her richest suitors, and she sings each night in the salon as if she sings upon the stage of the national opera.

Each night the salon rings with applause – and if applause is not love, then what is?

* * *

Ten years later – blink and you will miss it – that girl finds la Orpheline asleep in the costuming room and snaps the child's wooden crutches under the heel of her boot. She imagines the applause of the crowd as she watches la

Orpheline limp through the cavern of backstage, dragging her once-broken leg behind her, the roar pushing out the image of her benefactor embracing the perfect form of her rival, which is like a spelled knife in her heart. I mean, the tender piece of her heart that is left.

* * *

In the costuming room, la Orpheline and her fellow seamstresses crowd around a bolt of silk velvet held in the Costume Mistress's veined hands. How to describe such a color – the color of night? A blue that is nearly black, or a deep purple that is nearly blue.

Le Peletier's next production is to be Mozart's *The Magic Flute.*

Though the Soprano's performance as the Countess in *Figaro* was applauded, it was the new girl in the role of Susanna whom the newspapers praised and about whom *les patrons de l'opéra* are still gossiping. In next season's production, this new soprano will play the lead role of Pamina, while the Head Soprano – soon, she fears, to be head no more – has been pushed into the role of Pamina's mother, the mysterious Queen of the Night.

The base of the gown for the Queen of the Night will be made from that stunning velvet.

Black net will cover the full skirt and form the fitted sleeves of the gown, net which will be studded with flashing glass diamonds in silver settings shaped like stars. A long velvet cape, lined in the feathers of a thousand birds, each dyed a raven black, will be pinned to each shoulder with more faux white gems. And to crown the costume, a headdress of hammered silver and gold fashioned into silver stars climbing towards a golden half moon.

La Orpheline's hand trembles as the seamstresses stroke that new bolt of velvet, the other girls' exclamations of delight fading away to nothing behind the roaring in her ears. Something about the night-colored velvet reminds her of the soft fur of her catskin, and she still expects, as she has since *Figaro's* opening night, that any day there will be a knock on the stage door, and the Costume Mistress will come find her, the Magician looming behind her like a god of death.

When someone does finally come for her, it is not who she expects.

* * *

There's no need to change the set. Look, we're in the costuming room with la Orpheline again.

"Your mistress thinks I have come to see that you are well," la Reine des Fées says.

Did you expect her to be there?

"I told her that I saw you fall, on opening night, and was wracked with worry for your health."

Her gloved hands are folded in front of her dove-grey skirts, the feathers of her hat nodding towards la Orpheline as she gazes down with those astonishing eyes. The two of them stand alone on the bare floorboards in the center of the room, floorboards that are still scattered with snippings of cloth and clipped threads. La Reine des Fées has just confidently ushered the Costume Mistress and the other seamstresses out of the room and closed the door in their astonished faces.

"She thinks me eccentric. We must be quick, or she will wonder."

La Orpheline stares up at her, wondering what new sort of trap this is.

La Reine des Fées draws in a breath. "I have come to make a bargain with you. You know that your head soprano is my rival for my patron's affections, yes? I hear that she is to play the Queen of the Night in your next production. A role I know well." La Reine des Fées quirks her lips. Look how she can still laugh!

"I have received voice training, but unlike her, I am too well known in my current role to ever take the stage. Such has long been my dream," la Reine des Fées shrugs her thin shoulders, "but it seems such a thing is not to be. Not without your help."

La Orpheline is surprised but still wary.

"I have come to ask you to help me take her place on opening night."

Listen closely: la Reine des Fées' speech is a touch too fast, and serious, now.

"You must restrain her somehow – I do not care how – and let me in through the stage door. It's a full costume, I know, with makeup and a wig – you'll help me dress in it, and do what tucks and pinnings might be needed before I go on."

La Orpheline studies la Reine des Fées' figure, comparing it to that of the Soprano, her face carefully blank to hide the fast rhythm of her heart. She nods.

"But there is a second part to my request," la Reine des Fées warns, her dark eyebrows drawn together. "This gown for the costume, you must put into it everything you have, do you understand? When I stand on that stage, the Magician must see no one but the Queen of the Night, and he must fall blindly, hopelessly, in love."

La Orpheline starts.

"I know what you are," la Reine des Fées says. "And I know what he is. I have been where he lives." She shudders. "I have seen what he keeps there. And I have seen where he keeps it. Do this for me, and I will tell you where."

La Orpheline's heart pounds.

Look, on the other side of the door. The Soprano crouches with her ear to the thin wood, her body shaking with rage.

La Orpheline raises her eyes to the ceiling, turns her palms up as if to say: "How do I know you will keep your promise?"

La Reine des Fées opens one of her gloved hands. Inside is a little iron key with three wicked teeth. La Orpheline takes it from her. It is like ice in her hand.

"This will get you inside, and past his spells and wards." La Reine des Fées smiles a tight-lipped smile, the smile of a soldier. "I have convinced him to trust me."

* * *

A montage – for we are not bound by the traditional laws of physics and the theater, and there is much to see, now.

The seamstresses bent over the dark velvet and black net of the gown for the Queen of the Night, la Orpheline's lips moving soundlessly as she sews, the soft fabric and the flashing needle slipping through her fingers like dreams. While the other girls are engrossed in their work, la Orpheline pricks her finger with the needle, beads of her blood disappearing into the thick, dark cloth.

La Orpheline working in secret in her hidden bed at night, with fabric scraps she has slipped into her skirts. The stump of a candle stolen from backstage flickers with light.

The Soprano sneering at la Orpheline during a fitting for her gown, twisting this way and that in front of the costuming room's mirrors.

"No, it's not right at all," she says, and she smiles at la Orpheline. "Rip the stitches out and do it again."

La Orpheline pricking her fingers again and again, until callouses form on their tips, bubbles of blood trapped beneath the hard skin.

* * *

Act IV: The Monarchy of Broken Cages

Imagine a courtesan standing alone upon a dark stage. She is called "La Reine des Fées," the Queen of the Fairies, a queen of dreams and fantasies. They say that every king in Europe is dying to have her, and that she's turned each of them down.

She laughs – she can still laugh – because that is a stretching the truth a bit.

Still, the courtesan knows a cage when she sees it – she shrugs – or so she thought, and a king would be the smallest and strongest cage of them all.

So she chooses her suitors carefully, and she keeps a hidden cache of money set by, and she flatters herself to think that she might leave any of them at any time.

And then she meets the Magician – a cloaked and masked man steps onstage, spins her around – and realizes that all along she's been stupid and blind.

The scene changes – black-costumed stagehands push onstage the trappings for a lavish set of rooms – her new apartment off the Rue de Lafayette, of which the exact whereabouts are still unknown. Actresses dressed as maids wheel across racks of furs and elaborate silk gowns. One walks by holding up a priceless collar of diamonds. Look – wearing it must be like choking on ice.

The Magician pays for it all – and leaves her alone for days and sometimes weeks on end, and if she shudders when he touches her with those thin white hands, well, some men mistake that for desire.

And that is the most dangerous cage of all, the only one she's ever fallen into.

The one that at first looks like freedom.

By the time the scene changes again, to those dank rooms he still calls home – so different from her bright, comfortable apartment! – by the time he lays out his mouldering books in front of her, dangles that gruesome catskin in her face, his eyes alight with the gleam of madness, it's far too late.

She is caught, as sure as if she'd been thrust into the wire cage that glints under a spotlight in a corner of the stage, a tuft of brown fur still caught in its door.

He tells her of the girl it once belonged to, his voice filling with pride at his brilliance in catching her, with righteous fury at her escape.

And then she's at the opera, on *Figaro's* opening night, and a spotlight catches the girl falling from the rafters like an angel, and the Soprano glares at them as she sings, and the courtesan begins to see a way to free herself from this cage.

If she wanted to secure the Magician's love for her, she'd not have made plans to dress as the Soprano.

* * *

This story ends at the beginning. Opening night.

The magnificent gown for the Queen of the Night rests on a dressmaker's dummy in the center of the costuming room, finally complete, stitched together with la Orpheline's dreams.

Inside one of the hollow gravestones where la Orpheline sleeps rests a little gown of her own, sewn from the scraps. A long velvet dress, the color of night. A gauzy veil of black. She saved some of her power for this, so that when she leaves the theater she may travel unseen. Under cover of night.

And now it is time.

An hour and a half to final call, the costuming room is a maelstrom of frantic last-minute preparations. La Orpheline passes a note to the other seamstresses, calling for urgent help in the hand of the young soprano who plays Pamina. When they file out of the room, their skirts swinging, La Orpheline stays behind.

The Head Soprano enters the room, already in her makeup and wig, for the final fitting of her gown. She does not seem surprised to find only la Orpheline there.

Look: she has brought the Costume Mistress with her.

"I'm still unsure about the fit of this gown," the Soprano says, shrugging out of her silk robe. "I thought we might need the Costume Mistress's help." She smiles triumphantly at la Orpheline.

La Orpheline begins dressing her in the gown, her heart pounding in fear.

"Where are the other seamstresses?" the Costume Mistress asks, her brow furrowed in confusion, as she moves forward to help.

"Yes, la Orpheline," the Soprano says, "Where?"

La Orpheline shrugs as she fumbles with the row of jet buttons at the gown's back.

The Soprano scowls at her reflection in the room's mirrors. "Part of your plan?" she asks, and her voice is dangerous.

"What?" the Costume Mistress asks in surprise. "What plan is this?"

The Soprano sighs dramatically and turns to face them. "I do not like to say so, ma'am, but this girl has been using lies and subterfuge to steal from the company."

The Costume Mistress cuts her eyes back and forth between them, as if weighing the worth of the company's Head Soprano against that of a friendless little girl, and not particularly liking the math. "Our Orpheline?" she says.

La Orpheline looks down at the floor, her heart racing. Look, you can see her plan, slipping away through her empty hands.

"Look at me!" the Soprano shrieks, and she grabs the girl's chin. La Orpheline meets her eyes, her face set, as the Costume Mistress gasps.

"I have seen her," the Soprano says. "She has a key to the backstage rooms," and she loosens her grip on la Orpheline's chin to grope at her chest, finding the little iron key that hangs there. She tugs at it and the thread it hangs on snaps.

She hands la Reine des Fées' key to the Costume Mistress. "You see?" she says, and she smirks at la Orpheline, who is rubbing her neck.

The Costume Mistress turns the key over in her hands. "I do not recognize this," she says, and she glances at la Orpheline. "I will take it to the Theater Director, and see if he knows it." She speaks sternly to la Orpheline. "You will stay here."

"Have one of the dressers finish helping you," she calls over her shoulder to the Soprano as she turns and leaves the room, her face drawn into a confused frown.

La Orpheline watches as her key disappears.

The Soprano turns around, as if to gloat, and la Orpheline reaches behind her to the little toilette table and the porcelain jewel-case there.

She smiles as she breaks the case over the Soprano's head.

* * *

"You're late," la Reine des Fées hisses when la Orpheline opens the stage door, her breath coming fast in her chest. "I thought you'd abandoned our plan."

La Reine des Fées is dressed as an orange seller and swathed in a long cloak, but look at her eyes. Anyone who saw those would know her at once.

La Orpheline mimes singing, pretending to flutter a feathered fan at her face.

"The Soprano?" La Reine des Fées' eyes flash.

Forty-five minutes to final call, La Orpheline and la Reine des Fées are weaving through the panicked crowd backstage, la Orpheline's right foot dragging. Between the commotion of opening night and a missing soprano, no one looks at them. They slip into the costuming room, and la Orpheline turns the lock on the door.

"You have done as I asked?" la Reine des Fées says, and begins to hurriedly undress

A smile flashes across la Orpheline's face. Her hands had shaken as she stripped the gown and wig from the Soprano's body, as she gagged her and tied her hands with silk, but now that it is over she feels only triumph. The Soprano is stuffed into the costuming room's closet, and with luck it will be a while yet before she awakes.

La Orpheline makes shooing motions with her hands, urging la Reine des Fées to hurry. The Costume Mistress and the Theater Director could be back at any time.

La Reine des Fées frowns at her as she steps out of her dress. "Has something gone wrong?"

La Orpheline mimes a key turning in a lock, throws her hands in the air and looks around frantically to show the key lost.

La Reine des Fées quirks an eyebrow and looks the girl up and down. "*C'est dommage.* Then you must hope your leg is strong enough to kick the door in."

La Orpheline curtsies, somewhat ironically, her face turned towards the ground.

La Reine des Fées gasps when la Orpheline draws out the Queen of the Night gown. The girl helps her into it, deftly pinning the velvet tight at the waist. Look how it fits her perfectly, how the stars flash as she spins. "*C'est magnifique!*"

La Orpheline drapes the feathered cloak around la Reine des Fées' shoulders and settles the dark wig over her tell-tale brown curls. The moon-and-stars headpiece shines from the dark strands.

La Reine des Fées draws her own ivory *maquillage* case from the folds of her cast-off cloak and paints her face herself, applying kohl to her conspicuous eyes.

La Orpheline feels a surge of pride as la Reine des Fées turns in front of the mirror, transformed.

She holds up one finger. *Wait.*

La Orpheline cuts a piece of black net from the remaining bolt with her shears and spreads it over la Reine des Fées' wig, removing the headpiece and settling it back over the net to anchor it down. La Reine des Fées' face is now wrapped in darkness and unrecognizable.

La Reine des Fées finds la Orpheline's eyes through the net. She holds them for several heartbeats, and then she nods, as if satisfied, and presses a piece of paper into la Orpheline's hands.

"Do not worry about the Soprano, *ma petite amie.*" La Reine des Fées smiles grimly through her veil as she turns to leave the room. "All villainesses get their due in the last act."

* * *

Let's go out into the theater now, before the crowd is seated.

The orchestra is finished tuning. The house lights are on. The theater doors will open soon.

Places, everyone. Places.

The show is about to begin.

A stagehand walks through the wings, announcing the final call, and the Queen of the Night sails out to join the other singers, to the production team's audible relief. Meanwhile, la Orpheline is hobbling past the Costume Mistress and the Theater Director hidden in la Reine des Fées' cloak, on her way to her graveyard bed.

On the other side of the curtain, the doors open and the audience floods into the theater.

The Magician slips into his box, still cold with anger from the brief note he received that morning from la Reine des Fées turning down his invitation to join him. "I'm afraid I do not feel well, *monsieur,* and so I must decline..."

Look: the house lights are going down.

The orchestra plays the overture as the stage lights come up.

The curtains whisk open.

An hour past final call, the Queen of the Night steps onto the stage, in a gown so lovely that anyone who looks at her must love her, and the Magician is looking. La Reine des Fées' face is still swathed in her dark veil, and when she opens her mouth to sing, she leaves it down.

An hour and ten minutes past final call, the Soprano spits out her gag and starts to scream, but no one can hear her, not yet.

An hour and twenty minutes past final call, la Orpheline is hurrying through the dark streets of Paris, clothed in night, dragging her right foot a little behind her left.

There is a forgotten door in the Magician's house: the little door to the cellar, hidden against the house behind the weeds. Her leg is not strong enough to kick the door in, but she won't have to. When she escaped that way, she left it unlocked.

Of the many things the Magician never imagined, perhaps the most detrimental was that neither she nor anyone else would brave this door. Why place wards on it, why check the locks, when no one would dare enter the cellar, would walk past his ranks of caged and bottled servants, through their shrieks and their staring eyes?

And if they did, would his servants not warn him, would he not hear the noise, even if he was miles from home?

Only the most desperate, only a fellow demon in chains, could do it. Only she would they have watched silently with round eyes and cheered with squawks of joy and admiration when she pushed the door free with her shoulder, inch by grudging inch, dirt and silt streaming through the creeping fingers of sunlight.

A scrap of paper is clutched in la Orpheline's hand as she runs now, or tries to, through the Paris night: "Front hall, reach deep between the jaws of the stuffed bear head. Look inside the black silk bag, for the plain wooden box which contains a little clay pot which holds an old leather pouch. Ignore the golden jewel chest and the Fabergé egg. He keeps demons and spirits in there."

She is going back, and she will not ignore the jewel chest or the Fabergé egg. She will not leave the bottles corked and the doors closed.

"Break the cage while you're at it," the paper says.

The Pendulum Moon

Laura Hennessey DeSena

The men, like moths, rise from the darkness toward the lights. They emerge with faces that are pale and distant as the moon. The houses on the hill shudder as the miners gain the high ground, almost in unison. Their steps are uncertain and awkward—men who slip under the earth's surface like a second skin.

Mary watches the pendulum moon tick the time. Day passes quickly, busy with chores. The night is different. A crescent moon slices winter sky. Strip mines for picking coal and sinkholes that swallow houses: a landscape that awakens a darkness—in her heart, in her heart.

Mary's mother, too, waits. It is the waiting she and her daughter share, listening for sounds of the men returning from the mines in the hollowed out spaces between the slat boards. She is too afraid to go to the threshold before the sounds reach her. It is not the wind. It is not the wind.

No change with company money—credit and debt, these are the cycles. No pennies to rub together. No pennies to toss in chance. Nothing is wasted—flour sack dresses and potato dolls. Flour dough to twist into figures.

The parlor is sparsely furnished, in fading, somber colors. The outside door for formal occasions, like a wake, opens into the parlor. Beyond the outside door is a porch, rarely occupied—no time to sit in the sunlight. The true door to the outside is in the kitchen.

Mary sits on the wooden floor, the darkness settling around her. She has made a circle using pieces of coal, black stones, around herself. She is humming.

She is always waiting. From the moment her father leaves the house, in the midst of daylight chores, of picking coal down at the strip mine, of picking huckleberries, of picking mushrooms, of picking flowers, she is waiting. Her daily movements tick away the time—kneading dough and making beds, the sure motions reign in the uncertainties. Then her dog comes running through the huckleberry bushes, a snake wriggling in his mouth, a gift for her. They have not come home, not yet.

A sound, like a faint knock at the outside door. Mary rises from the center of the stones toward the door and opens it to emptiness. No one there. Mary moves back to enter her circle, taking care to step over and not on the stones.

Her mother's fear is tucked into the recesses of a faint smile. She places a heavy bucket of coal on the floor, wipes her hands on her apron.

Mary does not look up. "It's too dark to see."

"If you crack the window a bit, you might hear them coming up the hill."

"It's too cold to crack the window. And I don't like to listen for them. I like to see them coming up. I can in the spring and summer, while it's still light out. Not now, not in winter."

"You didn't hear the whistle, Mary?"

"If the whistle went off, you'd have heard it in the kitchen."

Her mother rubs her arms mechanically, remembering the cold, not feeling it now.

"I thought I heard someone on the porch, before."

"Not your father?"

A whisper that rises and falls on each breath.

Her mother looks toward the coal bin in the shadows. She moves toward it and empties the bucket of coal into the bin. The noise awakens them into keeping time again. Mary dispels its ticking with her voice.

"Listen, mother, it sounds like a song: *black stones, black stones, he gathers the hard coal from the dirt.*"

Her mother looks toward the parlor door, a strange straying in her eyes. Mary's father always uses the kitchen door instead. No one uses the parlor door. Not a threshold for the ordinary, not the parlor door. "They pulled my brother from the darkness. To die like that in a black hole... To work like that in a black hole... Too much to ask of men. Death is enough when it comes. Why seek it where it crouches and waits?"

"Do you remember the night of Uncle Johnny's wake?" asks Mary. "Your cries circled around my bed. I got up to see him in the coffin, here in the parlor. The candles still burned 'round his crushed body. When I came down the stairs, I could see him lying there—still and silent. As I touched down on the bottom step, he sat up."

"He sat up?"

"He sat up in one sudden movement, as though he just woke up and remembered something. Or heard someone calling him. Or heard me on the steps."

"Mary, what are you talking about? A dream?"

"No, not a dream. He sat up, straining to hear, and heard nothing. Then he fell back asleep. But, in the morning, at his funeral, he had forgotten us. What more could he do in this world?"

"I won't have you saying such things, Mary. It's sacrilegious. Sometimes the body convulses after death. I saw it once during a funeral. My grandfather, lying in his coffin. His arm suddenly jerked up and fell down again at his side. A woman in the church cried out and the priest came rushing down from the pulpit to calm her. Uncle Johnny's body convulsed—his muscles fighting the long sleep."

Mary goes to the parlor door and opens it, and the darkness in the room exchanges places with the darkness of the night. She is listening. But it is really to escape the room for a moment that she stands in the doorway, asking, "Did you hear...?"

"No, but go and see. Pray it's not the Black Maria going up the hill."

"No, nothing, no faraway sounds. And I haven't heard the group of them pass by. I thought I heard a knocking at the door."

"And not your father?"

Mary closes the door and leans with her back against it for a moment. "It's the cold seeping into the door. The wood is groaning, is all." Mary recites what she has been humming, a song taking shape in her head: *The men like moths let loose on the night, rise from the valley toward the lights.*"

"What are you talking about, Mary?"

"There is some beauty just in words, in the sounds they make."

"Mary, how can it be beautiful to breathe black dust all day and listen to explosions echoing off walls and the roof timbers shaking like they're about to come down and crush..."

"Listen." Mary rises in one fluid movement from the wooden floor. The humming in her head is louder now, and it spills out into words: *"Waiting, listening for voices in the throb of the wind, in the shudders of the house."* Mary listens to the house.

"That sounds like words you'd sing. I will say that."

"At night, waiting, you talk about death—the man who hanged himself on the tree in the woods," says Mary.

"I had to pass that tree on the way to work in Coaldale. My sisters were with me and we were all afraid when we came to that spot. We jumped over the place under the tree. We wouldn't let our bare feet touch down on that spot."

"Or hunting accidents. Or coal miners trapped in the mines."

"Always coal miners trapped in the mines," says her mother. "My whole life has been spent listening for the whistle. Worrying about my father, then my brothers, and now..."

Mary looks toward the window by the front door. "There's someone on the porch, Mother."

There is a single hollow rap on the door.

Her mother rises from her chair. "Your father?"

Mary opens the door to see out onto the porch. "No, no one. No one is here. No one is there."

Her mother sits back down slowly, reluctantly. "The wind." Her mother says this tremulously; it has not quelled her fears.

"Imagine no wind, no air in the shafts."

"It finds them in the shaft, but it must be a faraway sound if you are deep in the mines."

"A welcome sound."

"The fire is dying out."

"Mary, put more coal on the fire. I have to set the table for supper."

Mary gets up to put coal in the stove. The bin is getting low and downstairs there isn't much left to carry up. "I can pick coal down the strippings tomorrow—before school."

"I worry about your getting caught, Mary. I heard the sheriff is watching the slag heaps. What, will he arrest children for picking coal to stay warm?"

"Enough to keep us warm through the winter."

"You save us company money," says her mother.

"Company money isn't real."

"What's real then?"

With the final beat of her last word, a loud knock is heard on the door.

Mary's mother stands up in front of the chair, but does not move toward the door.

"I'll see who it is, mother."

Her mother is rooted to the floor. "Something's wrong, Mary. They say that three knocks and no one there means death is come to announce its arrival."

"Don't say that. Open the door and see who's there."

"I can't. Mary, you go. My legs are stuck in this spot."

Mary opens the door.

A broad-shouldered man stands on the threshold, holding his cap in his hands. "I'm Ian Thompson, the company man, Miss. I need to speak to your Ma."

Her mother sinks into the hardback chair as Thompson enters behind Mary.

"What's wrong?"

Mary moves behind her mother's chair and the man walks in front of the chair, facing her mother. He hangs his head as her mother moves to get up out of the chair.

"Go upstairs, Mary. I'll call you if you're needed."

Mary lingers a moment and then moves toward the stairs. She climbs them slowly, without looking back. She knows the story of Lot and his wife and she will not be tempted to add to the inauspicious signs of the night.

"It's a hard thing to tell, Mrs."

"No. No. Don't say it. Please don't say it." Her mother moves to stand at the window. She sees herself as though she has stepped outside into the night. She wills herself to speak, thinking of cold metal pickaxes and lunch tins, and boots waiting by stairwells. "But the whistle? I didn't hear the alarm go off tonight. Though I felt it—the sound."

"No, Mrs. No whistle. You're right. Orders were not to use it—only one missing and not too deep. The whistle brings the town to the mine and we didn't want to..." The company man raises his head to look at Mary's mother. He waits for her to speak, and when she does not turn to him, he rushes to be done with it. "You were expecting me, then, when he didn't come home." And then he looks down again, at his boots. He will not meet her eyes. "I left it. I left it on the porch because of, because of your girl. Too much dynamite. Not your husband. Another man, a careless miner it was that caused it. No blame belongs to anyone but the miners. The desire for a large haul is too great. Not your man, not your Danny. I am sorry that he, that he... I left him, I left it on the porch, Mrs.— because of your girl."

It had become his refrain. He had told this again and again to the women of the households. He was an unlikely dark angel, an odd banshee in his company suit, a crumpled man even for his broad shoulders. He was reluctant to see the children at all. They were always sent from the room and the woman bore the brunt of it alone, their shock bouncing the words back at him—their bodies were like walls and the word echoed in the room. Pieces of a man are not a man. How can you identify what you cannot place—what you do not remember? Dust to dust and forgotten.

"Wasn't I there when they carried my brother in—what was left of the man?"

He could not follow her meaning because of the echo. It was her husband he had brought home to her, not her brother. Without comprehending, he said merely, "I'm sorry, Mrs."

"Don't speak to me of your sorrow. Empty. Empty words." She looked up at him. "Leave my house."

"But I've also got to tell, you must know..." He crushed his cap in his hands. "Tomorrow morning..." Mr. Thompson looked down at his crushed cap. These were the lines in the scripted verse that he hated most, that had to be said, had to be said with an authority beyond question: "...you'll have to be going."

"Going?"

"Yes, Mrs."

"But my sister-in-law, she had, she had a few days."

"Times are harder. More want work. Men waiting for the spot."

"But how can I?"

"Company property. A new man to fill the spot down the mines. Plenty around looking for work." It was easy to fall back on the lines he had committed to memory. He felt himself gathering the strength he needed for this.

"His spot. The grave. You move him from one hole into another. You put another man in the ground and another."

"It's on the porch, Mrs. I didn't want your girl to see it."

"You left it in the dark?"

"I have to be going, Miss, Mrs. Do you want me to get your priest? I have to pass the church. I'll stop to tell your priest. Father Boland, is it?"

"Am I to pack up tonight?"

"Yes, Mrs. You must."

"What about the burial? What about the laying out of the body?"

"I'm sorry, Mrs. There is no body. All that's left is..."

"Where?"

"On the porch, out of the light. Because of your girl. My own girl is about her age."

She stands up stiffly and moves toward the door. "I'd forgotten. No body. No time for a wake and no body to wash and dress."

"I've got to be going now, Mrs. I'll stop by the church."

"No thanks, my Mary can go for me."

He backs away from her, moving toward the door. "I'm sorry, Mrs."

"Take your sorrow with you. It has no place here."

Mr. Thompson opens the door to exit into the darkness he had let into the room.

Mary's step is heard on the stairwell as she comes into view. "Mother, what is it? What's wrong?"

"He's not... We have to leave this place tomorrow, Mary. He's not..."

"Where is Da, then?"

"He's not coming home, Mary." "I could feel you listening at the back of my neck, like a cold hand touching the nape of my neck."

"It isn't true."

"We'll go to my sister's in Coaldale. There's work in the shirt factory, where I worked as a girl. I didn't take it before because to walk there was three miles from Summit Hill. And you have to pass the burning mines to get there. You could slip down there and no one would know what became of you. So many open holes in the earth to fall down into. If that place isn't the image of hell, I don't know what place is!"

"Where's Da?"

"No, Mary. Don't ask me that. Not tonight, Mary. Not when it's, it's lying outside in the dark. That's what he told me.

Out there, out of the reach of light. Hidden so as not to break your..."

"He's not dead. When the mines collapse, sometimes all that is left is a pile of black bones and dust. Sometimes they cannot tell, only if he doesn't come home, if he never comes back to the house. And maybe then he is roaming like when the Daley boys left the mines one day, just stopped working."

"He's not comin' home, Mary. Your father's not coming home. That's what's true. That's what's real. What's out there on the porch can be touched, Mary. Even in here, I feel it. Can you not feel it yourself, Mary?"

"When I pick up the coal in the mornings down at the strippings, I think about him working under the ground. I think how he smells like the dark. Not the dark fear of being under the earth—not that kind of dark—but I think when he holds me, I can smell the darkness. Darkness does have a scent, doesn't it? It's fresh like dark earth, but heavier..."

"I don't know, Mary. I don't know. I must think about where we're going and what..."

Mary moves toward the outside window to look up at the sky. "When I let the man in, I could see the moon behind him. A sliver of a moon—slicing the dark sky, like the pendulum of a clock."

"A pendulum?"

"A pendulum moon. The moon keeps the time like a clock. It's a frozen winter moon—a pendulum that stops when the clock winds down."

"It's cold in here, Mary. Get more coal from the cellar."

Mary picks up the bucket by the coal stove and then leaves, descending into the cellar.

Her mother faces the outside door, but does not move toward it.

Mary returns with coal in the bucket. "Here, Mother."

Mary's mother goes to the stove, bends down, and begins to place the coal in the stove. Stopping suddenly, she holds out one piece of coal in the palm of her hand and studies it. "Look at the coal—it's dark and hard and leaves stains on your palms."

"'Dust thou art'," says Mary. She moves toward her mother and takes the piece of coal from her mother's palm. "The stone turns into fire. Like the transfiguration at Mass. The bread becomes the body. The wine becomes the blood."

"Mary!" Her mother takes the coal from Mary's hand.

"Shall I bring it in?"

"What, Mary? No, Mary, I cannot. I cannot, not tonight. Not until the fire goes out. Maybe in the darkness, I can bring it into the house. I cannot. I cannot make my legs move to go out there." Her mother staggers a little toward the outside door. "In the dark and see..." Her mother blesses herself. "God rest his soul."

"How can it rest? If he's dead, then his body is scattered to the dirt and picked up by the wind and brought home to us. It's not out there..." Mary gestures toward the outside door and beyond it to the porch, "in a box. Do you think that man could pick up what was? Can he say: *this*." Mary holds out her arms as though burdened. She opens the door to look into the dark. "*This*."

"Mary, maybe I should bring, maybe I'm wrong keeping it there." Her mother turns to get her coat and wraps herself tightly. "I am going to get Derry McCarthy to bring it in tonight."

"I see it, Mother."

"Where shall I have Derry McCarthy take it? To the church? Is it too late to take it there? No service, no service until the morning. No one but ourselves knows what is waiting to be done. The packing. Do I pack first, Mary? Are we to leave here, then? At once and together?" Her mother, in confusion, turns back, moving toward the staircase as though to go upstairs and pack their personal things. What was practical would wait, was always there waiting.

As her mother turns away, the sound of a heavy step on the porch startles Mary. But her mother continues toward the stairwell.

"Da?"

Her mother whispers from the bottommost step, "Get thee behind me, Satan." Mary's mother is frozen in place, with her back to the outside door.

A tall man enters the parlor. He is in work clothes, covered in soot from the mines. His voice is cold and rings hollow in his wife's ears. "I'm sorry I'm late comin' home, Anne. There was a man missin' tonight. We found him—not too deep he was, but completely covered, and to get him out took the night from us, and there was no help for it. He was dead. The roof collapsed on him. The seven of us—there were seven who stayed behind to dig him out—went out for a stiff whiskey afterwards at the Matrician's pub. Too much dynamite, that's what the company men keep telling us, but they encourage it! Be damned if they don't! They want the haul."

Mary is motionless. Anne remains standing with her back to the outside door.

Her husband stares at her back. "What's wrong? Are you are not pleased to see me home at last, Anne? It couldn't be helped. The night was stolen from us in a tragedy. A life lost." He is pleading into her back because she will not face him. "No alarm, Anne. The company wants it quiet with only one man gone, dead. They know the men are organizing. The union men are biding their time to strike with every death in the mines. Word has got out already without the whistle to tell it. Down the Matrician's pub, the men are talking, yes, and the informers are listening. Ian Thompson—there's your man for that business. He's surely an informer. Well, out with it, Mary. What has happened then, here, tonight?"

Mary points toward the porch. "We thought it was you— the company man brought..."

Her father follows the line of her finger to the porch.

"It's out there in the dark. Out there on the porch. He carried it here himself."

"To my home? To your mother! Anne! I'll kill the fool who told the lie." Softly to Anne's back, "It's all right, Anne. I'm home."

Her mother is sobbing. Waves of grief break against the silence.

"Who came here tonight, Mary?"

"Ian Thompson. He came. He left it outside on the porch."

"But here your man comes to the wrong door and the other family doesn't know a sorrow has descended upon their home." Her father turns to look behind him into the darkness. "I'll have to go. I'll have to... To them, to the company men, to the owners and their operators, we are nothing, and we are all the same, all the same faces under a coat of soot. I have to go. I can't just tell the bad news and run out of the house." He pauses to let his words find their way through the low notes of her sobbing. "I'm goin' now, Anne. Put out the fire and go to bed. I can find my way in the dark."

Mary gets the kerosene lamp by the stove and lights it.

Her father, only a silhouette, steps off the porch, like it is the edge of the night.

She stands on the porch, looking up at the sky. She traces the curve of the moon with her finger. "Da?"

He steps off the porch into the night as if he cannot hear her voice.

Mary looks up at the sky. "Time has not stopped, then. The moon, not a tethered kite floating in the darkness."

The moon not still, not grounded on the edge of a precipice, a cliff of black clouds. The moon is not swallowed in a hole in the dark. It swings into the night, a pendulum of a clock.

Mary looks back down the dark road, but she cannot hear her father's footfalls on the path, nor his boots on the gravel, sounds that would travel up to her on the porch. The song in her head fills the silence: "*And the miners, let loose on the night, rise like moths from the valley toward the lights.*"

Mary holds her white dress out and drifts across the porch, moth-like, then lifts the lamp. The front door is still open to the night. "*Not toward the pale lantern of the pendulum moon.*"

Mary holds the lantern high and floats across the threshold. She stops before the coal stove and stares at the flames. The song takes hold of her and she speaks the words out into the night: "*Not toward the moon, but toward the fire that singes their wings, that sings in their blood, that summons them underground where all sense and meaning of time drifts in echoes, eddies in pools of sounds, rhythms of picks and shovels, where explosions of dynamite make bones dance inside bodies in unnatural light, in fading light, in the absence of all light, the light in their eyes no longer burning.*" Mary drops her hands to her sides and is completely still.

Her mother, still in her coat, is coming down the stairs. "Mary, close the door. The cold air is seeping into every corner of the house."

Mary bends to pick up the lantern and slowly moves to close the door. She holds the lantern high and peers out onto the porch. She is struck by what she sees. "I see it, Mother."

"I remember how, when I was a girl, the dead came home from the mines—yes, in a box. What's sacred? I want to know that, Mary. What's sacred?"

"Out there, Mother, on the porch."

Anne stands beside Mary on the threshold, but does not follow her gaze. "I'm going for Derry McCarthy. Collect your things. Find my black dress hanging in the back of my closet— lay it out on the bed for me."

Anne exits and Mary waits until she disappears into the night. Mary puts the kerosene lamp down and drags the pine box across the porch into the house. She places it within the circle of black stones and slowly opens the box.

With These Hands:
An Account of Uncommon Labour

LH Moore

George-Town, District of Columbia: 1800

I t is with a trembling hand that I write this. Given the color of my skin and the simple life that I have led and tried to create for myself so far, many would be surprised that I could write this at all. A breeze from the open window overlooking the river port makes me pull my woolen blanket closer about me. It is usually more normal than not for this swamp of a place to be humid during this time of year. I am relieved to have an unusually crisp late summer night, but the chill I feel comes from another source.

The light of my candle is dimming, the tallow becoming low, but this must be recorded. I look at the trinket sitting before me on the windowsill. How it made its way to me is of no import, but the fact that it did at all is what drove me to tell this tale. I once bore arms in our war of independence and faced redcoats and fear itself, but this?

This is something else.

* * *

It was the year 1796. I heard someone singing in Gaelic in the distance, their notes strong and clear and filled with longing. So many working there were from elsewhere, with families and loves either left behind or the reason behind such toil that they endured. So many sounds in the night. So many sounds in that place we were creating. European and Black craftsmen, artisans, and labourers both free and bound, all had been working for years on a symbol of a new country--*our* country.

We still had much to do as we worked to build the President's mansion or "palace" as some had taken to calling it. It loomed over us all as there was nothing else like it around these parts. General Washington himself chose the site and even drove in the stakes with the Irish architect Hoban at his side. All around us, this new federal city was a collection of farms and rolling fields and still more infested marsh than town. When I would get the chance, I would take a moment from my bricklaying to sit up high on the unfinished second floor to enjoy the view of the Potowmack River as the sun began to set. The noise of the other workers--their shouts, exertions, and work-songs--ceased as I watched the colors settle on the shimmering water. Despite all of the din around me, for a moment and only a moment--even if only in my mind, I was surrounded by quiet.

* * *

"Simeon, come, you must join us," Eugene said, waving me over. His brother Clifford stood next to him and looked at me with a huge smile. Both were tall and a deep golden-brown color from working in the hot summer sun. Where Eugene was dark-haired and dark-eyed, Clifford was fair--his eyes gray and hair light. Both of them had easy laughs and I had worked with them almost since the cornerstone was laid in 1792. They had come with Williamson, the master stonemason who trained them as stonecutters. They had also worked at the quarry in Aquia, learning how to manipulate the sandstone blocks that would cover the bricks I was laying. Unlike I who chose this work, the brothers were on hire from their owner, a wealthy planter from across the river in Virginia near the quarry. Some, them included, said that this planter was also their father.

"When I am finally like Free Simeon here, I am travelling the world! I am going to hop on one of those ships like we see on that river over there and sail to places no one would even think are real," Clifford said, holding out an ale-filled tankard.

"We are going where there are beautiful ladies with silks and rubies," Eugene said with a grin, taking the tankard from his brother. "Hell, *we* can be covered with silks and rubies ourselves!"

"I have heard there are buildings even larger than this palace we are building that are encrusted with jewels and gold. I am going with my chisel and mallet ready!" Clifford said, passing the tankard to me. "What is next for you Free Simeon?"

I thought for a moment as I took my sip. "Maybe I will meet a nice, good woman and settle down. Be happy with her. Have children. Live a decent life."

"Here we are talking about silks and exotic lands, and this man is talking about babies!" The brothers started laughing, but Clifford's face then became serious as he looked me square in the eyes.

"We cannot go on like this Simmie. This building here means freedom, but I am not free. There has to be a way to not be bound any longer. It is easy to think of children when you do not have to worry about them being enslaved," he said.

"Why you chose to come down here from Boston and Philadelphia, I do not know. Why bring yourself <u>closer</u> to all of this?" Eugene said with a wave of his hand. "At least away from here we could be our own persons, so that when we finally settle down, our children can be their own persons too."

Two of the other labourers had been lingering nearby. A little too close given the things Eugene and Clifford were saying. One spoke up.

"That can be arranged, my friend," he said, clapping his hand on Eugene's forearm congenially. Wait...did no one else see?! The moment his hand touched Eugene's skin, the man's hazel eyes turned black. It was fleeting, but I am certain I saw it. How did no one else?

"Just talk, that is all. Only talk." Clifford said to them, understandably nervous. I realized that the second man looked exactly as the first--twins. Of a similar height with those hazel eyes and dark, wavy hair. He nodded to his brother and spoke, the language one I did not recognize.

"If you do change your minds, we will be at the small grog shop nearby," he said. He clapped his hand on Clifford, who flinched slightly. I could not believe what I was seeing. It happened again. A touch and blackened eyes. How were the Hope brothers not seeing this too?

As we watched them leave, we all seemed a bit shaken. "That was rather odd, no? Where did they even come from?" Clifford said. "You do not think that they will say anything do you?"

"I somehow get the feeling that they will not," Eugene said, still watching them as they walked off to the opposite side of the work site. He groaned slightly, touching his hand to his head. "Does anyone else feel a little unbalanced? Perhaps it is the ale gone to my head."

"I feel a little off too brother," Clifford said. "This place and its heat!"

"Are you going to go and talk to them?" I asked.

They looked at one another and then at me, "Of course! These liquor rations we get just will not do. We are only going to the tavern to refill our tankard. That is all." We all started laughing, but inside, I found no humor. Not due to what I heard, but what I saw, and what I saw? That I could not explain.

* * *

The grog shop was a plain wooden building with one room furnished with rough wooden chairs and tables. Eugene called out to a barmaid rushing by with tankards in her hands. The curls of her strawberry blonde hair were barely contained under her cap. She stopped to look at him and rolled her eyes. "The Hope Brothers. What are you two doing in here?" she said, handing the mugs to her customers before coming back over to us.

"How's business Mary?" Eugene said as she looked them up and down. "As good as it will be. Now Clifford, you can visit anytime. That brother of yours...well...and *you*."

Mary looked at me, her slate blue eyes laughing as I put my hands up in protest. "I do not know how these two have wronged you, but do not look at me. I am just here for the ale."

"Only teasing. As for that swill? You are more than welcome to it. Nothing personal love," she said with a wink at the barkeep, her husband Sean. A burly man with a long scar on one cheek, he just laughed at her joke and shook his head.

* * *

The brothers looked around and saw the two strange men sitting in the rear of the tavern. "Simmie, we will be right back. We would just like to speak to them. Hear what they heard and what they are talking about." Mary brought me my own tankard and I stood sipping as I watched the conversation from afar. Once again, the men clapped the brothers on the forearm where their sleeves were not covering their skin. From where I was I could not see if their eyes had that same strange effect. I continued to drink, still watching them, and soon all four got up and walked towards me. I started to go towards them as well, having already paid, but Eugene put his hand up and looked at me with a smile. Clifford was smiling at me too. "Take care. Watch yourself," he said, nodding towards me. I assumed he meant my ale and the speed with which I was consuming it and said "I have drink. I am fine!"

One of the men looked at me and asked "Friend, are you sure?" I could feel one of my eyebrows raise as I held up my tankard, waved them off, and watched them walk out of the door.

* * *

The following morning I awoke with a start, surprised to have slept in a bit longer. Normally, the brothers awoke earlier than everyone else and enjoyed forcing me to be awake with them. I got myself together and walked over to the small wooden building the brothers shared with some of the other workers. "Good morning, this toil is not going to do itself!" I said, using their customary wake-up greeting. Clifford came out first, after shaking his brother. They looked at me blankly for a moment, and then laughed.

"We must have had too much yesterday!" Eugene said, as Clifford nodded.

"Too much? Is there such a thing?" Clifford said, laughing.

* * *

We walked away from the rough shelters towards our work areas. My day would be a hot one spent at the brick kilns, and the brothers would be needed to help cut stone for the Scottish stonemasons and their apprentices. As they parted from me, I overheard one of them say to the other "So much stone to cut. And Fitzgerald is worse than Imhotep himself. Do you remember when..." and then their conversation trailed off.

Im-ho-tep?

Away from the gregarious brothers, I had a moment to think about their question regarding my future. Being free, I had a small place where I had been living in George-Town, but staying there would have made me expend quite a bit of time travelling to work in Washington City. It became more convenient to live close to the project with the other workers. My parents had seen to it that I had some measure of education and apprenticeship. I had been trained as a bricklayer and thought my skills would serve me well. But then the War happened and I ended up living in Philadelphia. I had not given that much time to thinking about what was next for me.

Perhaps I should have.

* * *

The year was 1799. I was happy to be working on the second floor. So much progress had been made. It would not be much longer until the stonework laid over the brick was completed. They were already debating the lime whitewash to be put over that as well. Work had begun on the roof and the exterior would be finished. As I worked high on the second floor I looked out over the work site area. In the north clearing before me I could see the brick houses Hoban had built for himself and his assistants and the simpler ones for the rest of us. I smiled as I took pride in hoping that someday when I was long gone, this structure I helped erect would remain.

There were many other things that I could have been doing, but for that moment, watching the Potowmack sparkle behind me as I worked was enough.

I was broken from my thoughts by Jack Smith, one of our foremen, calling up to me. I had another task to do and another labourer took my place as I made my way to the scaffolding. As I did, he began to scold one of the sawyers--a German fellow--for a minor mishap. You could see on the man's face how diminished he felt as the foreman's voice became louder.

I saw Eugene nearby as he came close to Smith. He acted as if he was clumsy and stumbled against the man, grabbing hard onto his arm as he did so. He held Smith's arm tightly there for a moment, and then righted himself. I could hear him apologizing profusely and I expected to hear the foreman scold him as well.

It never happened.

I saw Smith put a hand to his head and mumble, his words muddled and confused. He leaned against a stack of bricks for a moment before excusing himself and quickly walking away. I did not understand what I was seeing. The man below who was being scolded had been watching it all with a look of confusion as well. He looked up, saw me looking on, and hurriedly rushed away.

The next day Smith did not show up to his post at work, having said that he was too ill to be productive. It was suggested that he have some rest, as he complained of feeling depleted and lacking entirely of vitality.

I did not mention what I saw.

* * *

Months later, the building was now a gleaming white. We had been celebrating the exterior's completion with extra whiskey rations after a dinner of salt meat, bread, and tea from the camboose. I took a moment to sit by Eugene and finally got up the nerve to ask him what had happened. Especially given that he had taken quite a chance with what he had done. "I must ask you. The other month...with the foreman. What was that all about? That does not seem like you to interfere with someone else's reprimand."

I saw him shoot a look at Clifford before he answered, and said "This is not the first time. I have done it so many times for so many others before."

By night's end we had all consumed a lot, which made for loose tongues. So much so that even Eugene and Clifford's Virginia accents seemed to slip a bit. We told one another raucous stories, each one more outrageous than the next. But that night the brothers told fantastical stories of incredible columned temples and pyramids with steps, grand libraries, and other ancient places of wood, of stone, of earth. Of palaces and fortresses, humble huts, and gleaming, gilded domes. Of master builders and masons and soaring cathedrals.

"Realities can be both destroyed and made. We build because we can and it is what we have always done," Eugene said dramatically, holding his hands out with his palms up as we all cheered. "It is with these hands that we can create a new world such as this."

I wanted to blame it on the drink. I wanted to take it as more of their imaginings. Their dreams of a future denied. They asked me more about myself and the family of which I was now the only member. The places I had seen in my own travels that had led me to this point. I could not remember ever having a conversation of such depth with them before. Clifford watched me intently. "Simeon, are you sure you do not wish to see more yourself? You must want to be more than this."

"I am content with the life I have for myself right now, but only for right now. Perhaps I will return to Philadelphia," I said to him. "Although there is work here, I constantly find myself increasingly unnerved by the state of my enslaved brethren."

"As am I," he said. There was none of the strong sentiment of previous conversations as he said this, but in its simplicity I was reminded of my own fortune and status. He looked at me again, "There are many who would give anything-- including themselves--for a chance to be free, Simmie."

Our work on the exterior was done and much fuss was made when the Hope brothers disappeared. Their master would not be happy to have lost both the wages he made from them, as well as the skilled labour and training. There was much speculation as to how and when they slipped away, but I finally knew all was not as it seemed.

Just before they left this gift currently upon my sill had been delivered to me--an exotic trinket from a land filled with rubies and silks. Upon its underside was carved the initials "E & C H".

It was then that I was certain.

I remember how the two of them smiled as they saw me with it, my face dumbstruck as I turned the bauble over and over again in my hands. I still do not know how it made its way to me, but it did. My voice quavered a bit as I whispered to them "What...what are you?"

A question they would not answer, saying that they had no answer.

To this day, even as I sit writing this account, I shall never forget the simple statement I was told when I asked my other question: "Why?"

"For freedom, we took their place."

The Song of the Iron Woods

Stephen K. Pettersson

T wo Northmen skied over snowdrifts made blindingly radiant by the sun. Sunshine lit up their beards and eyes while the arctic wind unmercifully bit at red cheeks and frozen ears. Before them were deep tracks that made craters in the crystallized snow, each oversized paw print lined with matted wolf's fur that reeked of urine and death.

The man with braided hair removed his glove, pushed aside his cloak, and reached to touch the edge of the outlines. After some time, he turned to his blood brother and pointed at the prints. "Be on your guard, Arne — we're getting closer. The Iron Woods shouldn't be far off."

Arne brushed the frost from his beaded beard, cupped his hands in front of his mouth, and exhaled powerfully to warm his face. He was eager to press on, but he had to be sure that they weren't following these beasts of horror for nothing. "You're sure she'll be there then?" he asked through deep breaths.

"No, but these tracks tell us that the part about the giant wolves is true. May it be just so that Angerboda makes her home there too."

The wind's gale rose to a flurry at the uttering of the giantess's name as if the very air shared in their contempt. In some ways it had every right to: the role her brood would come to play during Ragnarök would bring an end to not just the men and women of this realm but to the entire world as they knew it. She-Who-Offers-Sorrow was indeed both feared and reviled for the misery that was to come, but it wasn't for the future that these men hated but rather for the sorrow she had already caused.

"We need to find shelter before night falls... you won't find anything else in those tracks. Ulf?"

Ulf was pulled from his trancelike state by Arne's voice. He had heard something in the wind, something he had heard so many times before:

Sing for me.

It hurt to remember why they were here, but he couldn't stop himself from delving deeper into his memories; every single sound, scent, and feeling reminded him of *him*. At times, even the uttering of his beloved's name proved too painful, and so he kept it out of his mind and mouth. After a few breaths, Ulf turned to his friend and nodded. There would be a time for mournful reminiscence once they were safe.

The howls of the giant wolves echoed around them as they traversed the freezing terrain in search of someplace safe and warm. Ulf mumbled flattering words to Tor and to Oden to remind them of the sacrifices he and Arne had offered at the beginning of the journey and asked his gods to continue keeping them safe. It seemed to work, for no wolves or giants came to claim them as supper, and when the sun set in the sky, Tor swung his hammer into the clouds to illuminate their path with his thunderous lightning. Thanks to the storm, the Northmen found a small opening in the mountainside and made camp in the cavern it led to.

From the ceiling protruded sharp stalactites like the jaws of a hungry wolf, instilling an immense claustrophobia that was made all the worse by the lack of natural light. To combat the darkness, the men made a fire by the cavern's opening and warmed their frozen bodies as best they could. Ulf took to the dried meat and tore off chunks with his teeth while Arne sharpened his prized sword. The masterpiece shone brightly in its owner's hand, a natural fit in the man's large palm even though he had not crafted it himself. It had been a gift from Ulf's husband on the day before Arne's wedding to his wife — customary as traditions between brothers go, but still exceptional and extraordinary in quality. Ulf remembered how he could barely tear his husband away from the forge those last few weeks before the wedding.

"It has to be perfect," Ulf's beloved had said. "My brother deserves nothing less."

An uncommon smile streaked Ulf's lips as he remembered how long his husband had spent trying to get the rune of Tyr on the handle just right and how shy and uncertain he had been when he finally presented it to Arne. The joyous memory turned bitter as Ulf found himself longing for the man who forged it, a man who would never get to share in his smile again.

Arne must have caught his reaction since he stopped his sharpening and presented Ulf with the weapon. "I always think of him when I see it too. It's as if he is in the hilt of the blade when I hold it in my hand, as if he's behind the force of every strike I make and every drop of blood I spill. I'm not swinging the sword, my brother is," Arne said as he put the whetstone down and forced himself to their supplies despite his lack of appetite. Crumbs stuck to his beard like chicks in a nest as hunger and fatigue set upon him and he devoured the bread with newfound gusto.

Ulf took the weapon into his hands and weighed it pensively before responding, "I feel him in my arm too. Whenever I think of him, his arm ring tightens around my skin and I feel detached from it. Everything that I am becomes all that he was. It is as if he's haunting it, or at least I hope he is." The younger man paused as he recalled something amusing, but was in no mood to laugh. "Do you remember the uproar he caused when he gave it to me?"

Arne let out a hearty chuckle and almost choked on the crispbread in his mouth, "Of course I remember, I don't think anyone could forget the spectacle he made of it! Our kin certainly took notice—it was the only time the village ever turned against him."

Ulf shook his head and wagged his finger. "No, no, my friend. They could never grow angry with him — he was loved from the second he came into this world, and they never stopped loving him since. No, it was *I* that held their contempt. I took their legendary hero away from them, away from any children or legacy he might one day have." There was a bitterness growing in his voice that was directed at no one but himself and the guilt he felt over having loved so selfishly.

Arne placed his hand on Ulf's shoulder. "You were the only person my brother would ever talk about, and no man or woman could ever have taken your place." He paused and let go of Ulf's shoulder before continuing, "You know, he was always pestering me about introducing the two of you, and when I finally did, he wouldn't stop talking about you — how he wanted to hear your voice every morning, stand by you in every battle, and take you as his husband. He never cared about a legacy or children, and with time neither did the village, once he continued to prove himself."

"Except your father," Ulf scoffed resentfully. "He still cared right up until the end."

"Well, yes, but there is no pleasing that man. After I married Astrid, at *his* request no less, we never got a moment's rest. There was constant hounding about what we were doing wrong and how he would do it better. Maybe you were better off with my father's absence."

"Maybe. I think that's why your brother declared his love for me so openly. It was a challenge to anyone who would deny him his right to happiness. And like every challenger before and since, he bested them all, be it with words or with weapons."

Arne's mood became somber as he found himself wishing that his brother hadn't been quite so great a fighter. It was a terrible thing to wish for — the death of one's family at the end of a stranger's blade. But at least then he would have seen Valhall. At least then grief wouldn't eat at Arne's most cherished memories of him, forever tainting them like parasites in grain. He could make peace with a warrior's death, not one of sickness. Tears streaked his cheeks and soaked his beard. "I... I just miss him. I miss him terribly, painfully, with every moment awake and asleep. I wish I could sing for him again, if only the most ephemeral tune." He had never talked about his brother's death so candidly before and realized that he didn't know how to. It was a feeling so strong that words could never be enough to explain how he felt, no matter who spoke them or how they were told. Of all the mourners, only his blood brother could understand his tears and not judge them as weakness.

Ulf brought his friend in for a close embrace and rested his cheek on Arne's neck. "I know. I weep for him too, and at times I feel anger and hatred so consuming it's all I that I become." Ulf's voice came at first as a whisper but built into a steely conviction as he pulled away. "But we won't have to feel that way for long, and neither will anyone else that held him close. We will dry our tears and quench our hatred with the death of Angerboda, and we *will* have revenge for the mire of sorrow she's drowned our people in."

Finding strength in Ulf's spirit, Arne took up his sword once again and held it between them both in a tight grip. Through gritted teeth and glossy eyes, he spoke, "I swear on this remnant of my brother, on Tor and on Tyr, on my name and on my honor, that I will not rest until Angerboda's blood is staining the edges of this sword."

They held each other once more until exhaustion finally overcame them. As they drifted off to sleep, nightmares haunted their rest. The brother dreamt of his kin at a young age, playing together with him in the sand, far away from the stern eyes of their father. The husband dreamt of his lover in the Temple at Uppsala, lost in deeply devoted prayer as the sun cascaded across his face. In both dreams their loved one turned to speak, but before any words could come out, a thick, black tar oozed from his mouth and pores until there was nothing but darkness left.

The following morning they set off once again, leaving most of the provisions they had in the hideout. After only a few hours of walking, the snow-clad hills and chilling frost began to abate for unexpected greenery. Dandelions and bellflowers sprouted through densely packed snow and lush bushes thrived despite their frost-covered leaves. Tall oaks towered over the Northmen and filled them with unshakable unease. With only the first foot into the trees' embrace, they were knee-deep in a wide variety of bushes and plants that colored the forest with speckles of red, blue, and yellow.

"Is this it then? Is this the Iron Woods?" Arne asked with a cautious whisper.

Ulf tightened his braided hair and gripped one of his bearded axes so fiercely his knuckles whitened. "No, this isn't supposed to be here. It should be all snow and then—"

Something grunted and shifted in the bushes a few strides from where the two were standing. Panting and mumbling intermingled with the sound of metal clinking. Arne drew his sword and peeked around the nearest birch as quietly as he could, but couldn't see anything other than more green. Then the bushes moved and uncovered a woman. Waist-long brown hair and tattered clothes dressed her pregnant body while large, round earrings dangled from her earlobes. At first she looked so ordinary that he took her for just another explorer — maybe someone who had been wronged like they had? And then he saw her nose, followed by her tail.

Troll.

Ulf spotted her too and lowered Arne's weapon with his hand. "She's not a threat. Trolls usually aren't."

"Her child will be. Do you want another wolf or giantess in our world?"

Ulf wouldn't back down, "Of course not, but we'll deal with those when the time comes. What's more, the troll makes her home in the Iron Woods — she could lead us to Angerboda if we follow close. Don't rush into this, Arne."

Arne hesitated for a moment, but with an annoyed glance, he sheathed his weapon and sighed. The two men began moving again. They maneuvered silently over moss-covered rocks and fallen branches so as to stay in stealth while Ulf kept them downwind should the trollwife's nose prove to be more than just for show.

Humming an old lullaby, the troll tread effortlessly over the same passage that the warriors struggled to keep their balance on. Every once in a while she would stop in her tracks and fill her wicker basket with blueberries, lingonberries, and the occasional wild strawberry that didn't immediately go into her mouth. After some time she made a stop at an isolated snow mound in the middle of the thriving forest. Frowning, she stopped her humming and placed her hand over the abnormality while another tune took the place of the first. The melody resonated within the Northmen, vibrating their very souls and bringing peace to their minds, but it wasn't for them that she sang — they couldn't even understand her. Within seconds, grass and vegetation parted the snow and reached to tickle her stumpy fingers as a satisfied giggle erupted from the trollwife. Nothing but an echo remained of the frozen mound as fertile soil had completely taken its place.

At once Ulf understood how this lush forest could have sprouted from such a barren place. They watched the plants climb and climb until they could make out a fully grown juniper bush, standing tall in its berried dress. So utterly transfixed by the miracle performed were they that the trollwife slipped away unnoticed amongst the enveloping undergrowth. Panicked, they spread out and looked for the near-undetectable tracks she had made in the foliage. A tuft of hair here, indented moss there... it was little to go by even for someone as skilled in tracking as Ulf. After some time, the clues became more and more sparse until there was nothing to go by at all — not because she suddenly disappeared, but because there was no vegetation left to track *in*. Arne stared slack-jawed at the sight before him as Ulf took both of his axes in hand and spoke:

"*This* is the Iron Woods."

An intricate patchwork of metal plates buckled underfoot, absorbing the sun's rays until it was blistering to the touch and radiantly warm even through the men's shoes. Trees of copper, iron, and steel stretched towards the sky with sharp, pipe-like branches and perfectly symmetrical leaves that could cut a man open from head to toe come autumn. Unlike the frozen landscape that had preceded it, the Iron Woods could never thaw its plating or reinvigorate its soil. No fruit or life could ever grow in this grim and desolate place where impenetrable layers of iron had taken the place of earth. Only an all-consuming despair thrived in the woods that sheltered She-Who-Offers-Sorrow.

The two men had their weapons at the ready, waiting for any giant wolf, giantess, or trollwife that sought to cast them out or eat them whole. With unsteady steps they navigated a treacherous terrain where every flower, bush, and log had an edge so keen a simple touch drew blood. Arne misplaced his hand and a shallow but long cut expanded across his skin. He had suffered far worse injuries before, even on this journey, and so he didn't so much as grunt in pain. However, a feeling of dread and paranoia settled in his stomach as he began to doubt that he could uphold his vow to defeat Angerboda. How could he when the very trees worked against him, when every step led them towards a greater threat?

Ulf read his features and made a gesture for him to watch closely. He raised his hand dramatically, made a small nick in his skin with the edge of his axe, and then declared, "We are in this together. Where you go, I go. When you fight, I fight. When you bleed, I bleed." He pressed his sanguine palm into Arne's in a steady clutch that reaffirmed their blood oath.

"I have you and you have me," Arne agreed and smiled encouragingly, although he wasn't sure if even both of them were enough for what was to come.

A woman's ecstatic cry echoed close, drawing them from their intimate moment. They gripped their weapons once again and snuck closer to the sound's origin where a humble yet massive house of iron stood in an open glade. Two figures stood by the opening: the first was unmistakably the trollwife they had encountered earlier with her basket now open on the ground and filled to the brim. The other was a woman, taller than both men put together and then some. A crown braid circled her head, tattoos colored her muscular arms, and sad eyes juxtaposed the smile she bore on her lips. While no mountain would quake under her feet, and though she was not so tall as to touch the clouds, there could be no doubt that the woman was a giantess.

"Run along now. Your son will crown tonight, and you need all the rest you can get," Angerboda said with a deep and uncompromising voice. "The labor will be hard and bloody, but I'll be with you shortly to help with the delivery. Now go, I need to tend to some visitors." She waited until the troll had waddled out of sight before she continued speaking. "You can come out of hiding, assassins." The giantess spat out the words as if they held the essence of contempt itself.

Slowly and with iron at the ready, Ulf and Arne stepped into the glade's revealing light. Although her size sowed terror in their hearts, they still met her gaze, keeping their grief and vengeful scorn as a shield from fear.

"What wrong have I committed for you to draw your weapons so brashly against a giantess?" Her tone indicated that she didn't ask because she was insulted by the act but rather because she couldn't believe that anyone would dare defy her.

"Are you not Angerboda, She-Who-Offers-Sorrow?" Ulf's voice held steady even though every muscle in his body urged him to run.

"That cruel moniker?" Angerboda laughed sardonically in response. "I am Angerboda, yes. Warrior and witch. Mate of Loke. Mother of Fenrir the Great Wolf, Jörmungand the

World Serpent, and Hel, Queen of Helheim. Is that why you stare with such violent intent? For the crime of motherhood?"

Ulf clenched his teeth so hard he thought that they might shatter in his mouth.

In his place, Arne answered, "No. You took my brother from me. You brought grief to an entire village when you killed him, and now all we do is mourn. No more songs are sung, no children are born, and no one can bring him to memory without heartache. I've made a vow to bring you to justice, to sully my blade with your wicked blood."

Angerboda waved her hand dismissively at Arne's response and sighed. "Then you may leave, for I had nothing to do with the death of your brother. Your vow is null — there is no justice to be had here, only more grief. Coat your weapon in someone else's blood."

"Your name is more than just a moniker." Ulf's voice came harshly through gritted teeth while he closed the distance between them. "She-Who-Offers-Sorrow, Harm-Bidder, The One Who Brings Grief... They're not just names, but a way to define your being and the hatefulness you let seep into this world. It's a curse and a promise, one you have already fulfilled. Your cruel magic brought sickness to his lungs only so you could infest our hearts with your spiteful gift — that of eternal sorrow. You will die here, Angerboda, and with your death our grief shall end. Make peace with it."

The giantess took a moment to look the Northmen over, a frown forming on her forehead. She disappeared into her home while confused glances were exchanged between the two friends as they wondered what came next. Then she emerged, spear in hand and with a mien of sorrowful determination. She would stand and fight. "Come then, but know that I have given you another way."

As one, the blood brothers moved in. Ulf spun and slashed wildly with his axes in a lethal flurry while Arne's blade made precise cuts. Angerboda was bigger, stronger, and more experienced than either of them, but even she was kept on her heels against two synchronized fighters coming from different directions. Even so, all they could manage was a few cuts on her legs before her spear would come crashing down, always an inch away from splitting them into pieces. After some time, sweat and fatigue began to overcome the two companions while the giantess still fought with great ferocity. Angerboda was moments away from victory when Ulf's bearded axes hooked onto her spear and pulled it from her hands with all the force he had left. He pushed the attack but didn't get another blow in before a knife as big as his arm found his gut. Ulf stumbled back, the air knocked from what remained of his sundered lungs, and fell to the ground.

Arne, caught up in his own bloodlust and frenzy, didn't notice his friend fall. He saw only the opening presented by the giant's poor footing and pressed his advantage. Toppling her with a resounding *thump*, he moved his sword to her throat. He had but breached the surface of her skin when she cried out and pointed at Ulf:

"A life for a life! I can save him."

He paused and looked at Ulf, who was dying on the heated plates. Shock and guilt overwhelmed Arne as he realized what he had neglected in his vengeful battle. "How can I trust you?"

"It's that or he dies."

Angerboda didn't have to prove herself to him and she knew it; Arne would take the risk whatever she might have said — the alternative was unthinkable. Withdrawing his sword from her throat, he ran over to his friend and tried his best to keep him conscious.

Much to his surprise, Angerboda kept her word and began working on the injury immediately, despite Ulf's weak attempts to refuse her aid. She placed her hands over his gaping wound and began singing as she wagged to and fro. He began to twist, grunt, and gasp in agony as she worked her ancient magic on him. A few seconds later, sinews of flesh began closing the gory spectacle just like a seamstress would patch a hole in an old tunic. Inch by inch the healing took effect as the warrior began to recover from his wound. A gnawingly uncomfortable silence hung in the air as they waited for what came next.

Finally, Angerboda broke the tension. "I want you out of my realm. Now."

Arne sheathed his weapon and answered with what pride he had left, "I'll keep my promise as you've kept yours, but before that vow was made, I had already sworn on my name and on my gods to defeat you and—"

"Stain your sword with my blood, yes," she interrupted. "Was I not defeated? Is your blade not slick with my lifeblood?

"That's not what I meant, and I intend to keep my word."

"So change what you meant, the gods won't know. Moreover, wordplay is a favorite of theirs. There is nothing else for you here — your pain is not my concern."

"And what about our grief?" asked Ulf weakly. "What about the misery that hangs over our village since the death of my husband. Will you lift the curse?"

"Are you deaf, boy? I had nothing to do with what happened to your loved one, and there is no curse. My moniker has nothing to do with the misery and misfortune of mortal lives — it is but a cruel mockery of my motherhood. Your people won't sing for tears choke the songs in their throats before they're heard. No children are born for lovers' hands clutch weapons in delusional vengeance instead of each other. Sweet memories are tainted not because of magic, but because of your own eagerness to let them rot in the present. You've chosen how you grieve for him, not I."

For a moment it seemed as if they would concede the point to her reasoning, but before long, Ulf scoffed at her presumption. "And what do you know of grief, giantess? How could you possibly understand what sway true sorrow holds over one's mind?"

She bowed her head solemnly and closed her eyes as the inescapable washed over her in a flood of emotions. She sighed deeply and mournfully. "Come Ragnarök, two of my children will face gruesome deaths to the jubilant cheers of the gods' sycophants. All that I know them to be will no longer matter, only what history has deemed worthy of telling. Whatever you may think of them, whatever you may think of *me*, this is a sorrow that no mother bears lightly." Her voice began to shake, but still she continued, "I will speak no more of this, but hear me when I say that I know grief. It tugs at my heart at every waking moment and I dread the hour that I will inevitably lose them forever. But still I cherish and celebrate being their mother. I choose to embrace the good and I choose to embrace life. Hatred and despair will not save the ones we love, nor will sorrow honor their memory."

The Northmen didn't know what to say. Something felt right about what she was proposing, but they had no trust in her honesty. But, for the first time since his husband's death, Ulf lost himself in glimpses of their past together without an unutterable darkness taking control of his mood. Whenever he thought about his beloved before, there was always that incessant interruption of grief, like pricking oneself on the thorns of a bush when all you wanted was the sweet fruit that it bore. Now, there was still pain, still a thorn pricking him as he sampled the fruit, but for once he could do so without the taste of blood in his mouth. "And what now? What becomes of us?"

"For this night alone I will house you, but you shall be gone by the morning. You will never return here and we shall never see each other again. As for your grief... Only you can decide when you're through with fighting and mourning and when you're ready to live fully again. With this I will leave you."

She didn't give them time to respond before she vanished before their eyes. Arne rushed forward, looking for any trace of her that remained.

"She's gone, my friend," Ulf whispered gently.

"My sorrow isn't."

Ulf rose on unsteady feet and moved to embrace his blood brother, "Neither is mine, but I'm not so sure anymore that her death will accomplish anything. We need to let this go."

Arne didn't respond, but let himself be held for a moment, releasing the tension that had built in his body. The anger was gone, and in its place only an emptiness remained that waited to be filled by something more worthy of his brother's memory.

That night, the two blood brothers dreamt of their loved one as they had so many nights before. The husband dreamt of the early morning after their wedding, just as the sun had begun to rise but before either had made a move to get dressed. The brother dreamt of the two of them on the eve of their first raid, when the waves crashed around their boat and cries of anticipation filled the air. In both men's dreams, their loved one turned to speak, and from his mouth flowed words that they had heard so many times before:

Sing for me.

The Troll Sons of Grýla

Henry Herz

'T is rumored that the wizened troll Grýla ate her first two husbands, which perhaps explains the obsequious nature of her third husband, Leppalúði. Together they trod the stony halls of their dark Icelandic lava fortress, Dimmuborgir. Though gloomy and cold, Dimmuborgir never lacked noise or commotion thanks to the trolls' thirteen full-grown sons, who were so easily distracted and so eager to make mischief that they could only be relied upon to be unreliable.

"Samhain is nearly upon us," said Grýla, glancing out a narrow window at the waxing moon.

"Mannfólk now call it Halloween, dear," replied Leppalúði. "Over the centuries, their language changes and their ways meander like a frog chasing a swarm of flies."

"I trust the wisdom of the old ways," Grýla scoffed. "Come. Let us gather firewood in preparation for the Samhain bonfires."

Leppalúði sighed—softly, so as not to be overheard.

Grýla led her spouse to the entry hall, barefoot steps echoing in the rough-hewn passageways. Empty sconces left the room cloaked in menacing darkness. "Where are all the candles?" Grýla asked, turning in a slow arc. "Has Kertasníkir been at his pranks again?" She frowned. "His foolishness must stop."

"Now, dear," replied Leppalúði, as he laid a gnarled hand on his wife's shoulder. "You know how our sons love to make mischief of one kind or another. And remember, Kertasníkir has a taste for tallow. Have you ever chewed on a candle?"

"Certainly not," said Grýla with a scowl. "You know that the old ways forbid it. I can only eat naughty children that I collect on Christmas."

At Grýla's signal, Leppalúði raised the rusty portcullis. She led her husband through the front gate. Their breath fogged in the Október air.

Grýla's stomach rumbled, startling two crows into flight.

"How is your hunger, dear?" asked Leppalúði.

"Each night, I go to bed without eating anything," replied Grýla, putting her hands on her gurgling belly. "I've had no food since finishing my cauldron of kid stew at miðsumar. I snare fewer and fewer children at each Christmas. Woe is me. You have no idea what it's like to be famished for months at a time."

The corners of Leppalúði's mouth turned down. "Why do you suppose the Yuletide pickings have thinned?"

"I'm not certain," replied Grýla, shrugging. "But I suspect old Krampus is somehow at the root of this. Rumor has it that he has relocated from Merkenstein castle in Austria to the Rock of Dunamase in Ireland. I shall send Gáttaþefur to discover what new deviltry is afoot."

* * *

Two weeks later, a travel-stained Gáttaþefur returned from his spying. "Mother, you were right," he exclaimed, wide-eyed. "Krampus abides at Dunamase and has crowned himself Horned God of the Witches. The nearby coven at Sráidbhaile does his bidding."

Grýla lurched to her feet. "I'll wager Krampus sends his witches to snatch Icelandic children on Krampusnacht. No wonder they have become scarcer." She dismissed her son from the great room with a nod. "Did you hear that?" said Grýla, turning to her husband. "God of the Witches? Such arrogance! But the injury is worse than the insult. If his depredations continue unchecked, there will eventually be no naughty children in Iceland left for me."

Leppalúði nodded, his mouth a tight line. "But Krampus is powerful, all the more so with a coven aiding him. Do you dare oppose him?"

"On the contrary," replied Grýla, rising from a crudely carved stool. "I dare not ignore his threat, since I must be able to eat. Nor am I a foe with whom to trifle." She paced the cold stone floor, rubbing a hairy wart on her chin. "Krampus may have thirteen witch minions, but I have thirteen mighty trolls."

Leppalúði reached out a thick arm to calm his wife. "You would involve our sons?"

Grýla swept aside her husband's arm. "Krampus has added pieces to the chessboard, so I shall remove them."

"But how?"

"By kidnapping," replied Grýla, eyes wild. "Each of our sons will snare a witch. Tomorrow is Samhain, when the Veil between this world and the Otherworld thins. Our elvish allies, the álfar, can guide our sons to Ireland. Gluggagægir shall lead the raid. He is the least undisciplined of our brood."

Gluggagægir strode into the room at the mention of his name.

"Snooping again, eh?" observed Leppalúði.

"I prefer to think of it as keeping abreast of developments," replied Gluggagægir with a shrug and a grin.

"Regardless, I have need of your keen eyes, son," said Grýla. "Come, sit."

"Allow me to save us time," replied Gluggagægir, grabbing a worn stool. "I overheard your plan for Krampus's witches. It seems an unnecessary risk to me."

Grýla glared. "How is eating unnecessary?"

"Not that. But instead, avail yourself of the bounty of our lands. I can get you some svið."

"I devour children's heads, not sheep heads," said Grýla.

"What about hákarl?"

"Fermented shark? You miss the point," replied Grýla, shaking her head. "The old ways require that I devour only misbehaving children."

Gluggagægir took a deep breath. "But you could avoid a conflict with Krampus by adopting some... flexibility in your diet. The local hrútspungar is delicious."

Leppalúði winced at his son's recommendation of sour ram's testicles.

Grýla stood. Her look brooked no dissent. "I cleave to the old ways. This Samhain, the álfar will take you through the Veil to Sráidbhaile. Then let the wild hunt start. Bring me back thirteen of Krampus's witches. You are dismissed."

* * *

On Samhain Day, Gluggagægir shepherded Kertasníkir, Gáttaþefur, and his other unruly siblings through the dreary lava fields and past Lake Mývatn to one of the álfar's enchanted spots. The journey to a ring of rowan saplings took longer than Gluggagægir expected, his brothers easily distracted by beetles, rabbit kits, and other fresh fare. Each troll carried a large sack, an obsidian dagger, and loop of hempen rope at his belt.

Gluggagægir cleared his throat to get his brothers' attention. When that failed, he cuffed a few misshapen heads. "In order to preserve Mother's supply of yule children, we must capture Krampus's witches and lock them in the dungeon at Dimmuborgir."

"But won't the mannfólk of Sráidbhaile notice us?" asked Kertasníkir.

"No. They wear costumes on Samhain. Mother believes that is how Krampus's witches will mingle unremarked in the Sráidbhaile parade," replied Gluggagægir, looking each brother in the eyes. "We shall blend in as well. If we take care, Krampus will not know who has taken his witches and will be unable to retaliate." Gluggagægir bellowed, "We must do our best for Mother!"

His brothers roared their terrible roars and gnashed their terrible teeth, before stepping back at the sudden arrival of three álfar. Humanlike in appearance, save for their pale countenances and delicately pointed ears, the álfar wore deep-hooded tunics and breeches of mottled brown and green.

"Time is short," declared the tallest of the trio. "Form an inward-facing circle around me and hold hands."

Gluggagægir nodded and his brothers complied.

The other two álfar rhythmically paced around the circle of trolls, one clockwise, the other counterclockwise, chanting a deep-throated huldufólk spell to rend asunder the wan Veil between the worlds. A sudden cold wind rose. Rowan leaves swirled. An unnaturally thick roiling mist engulfed the sixteen.

The leaf rustling faded as if smothered by an enveloping blanket. Only the aeolian chanting of the álfar remained as they all crossed into the Otherworld. Though they were told the passage would take but a few moments, it seemed to the trolls that they sailed through night and day and in and out of weeks before arriving in a copse of holly on the outskirts of Sráidbhaile.

The trolls shivered. The sound of distant Irish singing carried on the night wind.

"Our thanks," said Gluggagægir, bowing to the álfar. "As you well know, trolls cannot abide the sun. We shall return hither before dawn."

The álfar nodded slightly and vanished.

"The village is that way," said Gluggagægir, pointing in the direction of the singing. "Spread out and good hunting."

At their brother's bidding, the mischievous trolls took separate paths toward town.

* * *

Gáttaþefur entered a field of barley, crouching low to avoid being seen, but leaving a trail of trampled grain in his wake. He had nearly crossed the plot when an enticing aroma wafted past the hairy nostrils of his abnormally large nose. *Oi! Is that freshly baked bread?* he thought. Possessed of the keenest sense of smell of all his brothers, Gáttaþefur tracked the scent to a modest bakehouse.

No smoke rose from the chimney and no light shone from the window, offering Gáttaþefur all the invitation he needed. He forced open the flimsy door with one heave of a heavily muscled shoulder and soon busied himself stuffing one loaf of barley bread into his smiling jagged-toothed maw and the remaining loaves into his sack.

* * *

Giljagaur clomped toward a nearby farm. The split rail pasture fence broke under his weight as he attempted to vault over it. The sharp crack of snapping wood startled a few head of cattle. He landed in a heap.

Giljagaur picked himself up and shook off the fence fragments. He spied a full-uddered Kerry cow. *Warm milk!* he thought. The thirsty troll gave chase and the cow fled toward the barn. Breathing heavily, Giljagaur entered the building and pulled up short. He smiled at two rows of milk jugs.

* * *

Bjúgnakrækir headed straight for town. But he forgot his orders when his gaze fell upon a tall shack with no windows. *What could be in there?* He moved to investigate, soon salivating at the smell of smoke. *A smokehouse!* He forced his way through the door without so much as a knock. His jaw dropped, for from the rafters hung more sausages than the simpleminded troll could count.

* * *

Grýla paced to and fro in the great room at Dimmuborgir, her brow furrowed. "What is taking them so long?" she asked Leppalúði. "I fear our impetuous sons are off indulging themselves rather than following orders. I must see this done with my own eyes."

Leppalúði nodded, possessing the wisdom and sense of self-preservation not to gainsay his strong-willed wife on so important a matter.

* * *

Grýla bid the álfar bring her to Sráidbhaile.

Grinding her stumpy stained teeth, she raced through the countryside, gathering up the unruly trolls with a series of increasingly agitated ear pulls, rump kicks, and head cuffs. Grýla's face flushed redder with each son, for while some hefted full sacks, none of the sacks held a captured witch. She marched them to a nearby field.

They mumbled their excuses.

"Be still!" Grýla ordered, staring into all their yellow eyes without blinking once. "Do you want your dear mother to starve?"

The thirteen trolls swung their downcast heads from side to side.

"Now, listen. Time is short," said Grýla, hands on her hips. "We shall join the rear of the Samhain parade, acting like mannfólk dressed in large troll costumes. From there, I will send you forward one at a time. Grab the first witch you see, toss her in a sack, and bring her to the copse where we first arrived. Any questions?"

No one spoke.

Grýla force-marched her sons into town, where they soon joined the tail of the costumed, torch-waving procession.

"Gluggagægir, you first," whispered Grýla, the ancient troll sweating and huffing from exertion.

Her son nodded and loped forward, sifting through the townsfolk for a witch.

The crowd wound through the narrow village streets and Grýla quickly lost sight of Gluggagægir. "Kertasníkir," she whispered. "Now you. Go."

Grýla deployed her sons in this manner until she marched alone at the tail of the parade. She slowed her pace and slipped away, making for their rendezvous point.

* * *

Gluggagægir hurried through the drunken revelers. He spied ahead a woman in a long black dress, wearing a pointed hat and brandishing a broom. *She's a witch!* He maneuvered directly behind her. As they passed an alleyway, he looped an arm around her waist and clamped a hand over her mouth. Gluggagægir pulled her out of the crowd and into the dark lane. He tugged his large sack over the witch and tied it shut. After heaving the sack over his shoulder, he weaved through the darkness toward the enchanted spot, a smile on his craggy face.

* * *

Kertasníkir advanced along the left edge of the boisterous crowd. Craning his neck, he spotted a witch directly ahead. He hurried forward.

As if warned by a sixth sense, the witch looked over her shoulder just as Kertasníkir approached. Her gleeful expression soured. She spun and gestured at the troll with a slim wand of alder wood.

Kertasníkir's muscles suddenly stopped obeying his will. He collapsed in a heap at the side of the road.

Celebrants, assuming he was simply overcome with drink, laughed and paid no further heed.

Someone pulled a hood over Kertasníkir's head. He felt himself dragged into a side street and his arms and feet bound, whether with thick rope or by magic he could not tell. A sharp blow struck the back of his head and he knew no more.

* * *

Stúfur, the shortest of Grýla's offspring, worked his way through the jostling crowd, eager to do his mother's bidding. Out of the corner of his eye, he noticed the dark shape of a witch eyeing him from an open doorway. He swerved from the crowd toward her.

The woman took two steps back into the building, the amused expression never leaving her face. The implication of the witch's lack of surprise or fear of a charging troll did not occur to Stúfur until he crossed the threshold, triggering a blinding flash of red light before all went dark for him.

* * *

Grýla paced back and forth at the enchanted spot in the copse, her heavy steps flattening the turf.

After a time, Gluggagægir, Giljagaur, Bjúgnakrækir, and Gáttaþefur joined her, breathing hard from carrying heavy bulging sacks.

"What have you brung me?" asked Grýla, rubbing her hands together.

Gluggagægir grinned. "A witch." He untied the rope securing his sack and dumped its contents onto the ground.

The woman in the long black dress sat up and shook her head to clear it. When she noticed five real trolls surrounding her, she fainted straightaway.

"An odd reaction from a witch," observed Grýla, scowling. She bent down for a closer look. "And that's not her real nose. It's a false one. This is no witch!" she cried. "What have *you* brung me?" she growled at her other sons.

They wilted under her glare. Finally, Giljagaur summoned the courage to speak. "Just jugs of milk I stole."

Bjúgnakrækir and Gáttaþefur offered similarly disappointing tales.

Her face the color of an Icelandic beet, Grýla raised her hand.

But before she struck, her son Askasleikir burst through the bushes. "They have seized Skyrgámur," he cried. "From a distance, I saw two witches cast a spell on him. He vanished."

Grýla's expression changed from anger to concern. She moaned and held her head in her hands. "And since they have not joined us, my other sons are also likely captives of the witches. How did they discover us?" Her eyes widened with realization. "Krampus! He helps the coven. We need aid as well."

With the thick fingers of her left hand, Grýla grasped a copper amulet hanging around her neck and chanted in a tongue unrecognizable to her sons.

The three álfar appeared.

Grýla turned to them. "Kindly conduct my five sons home to Dimmuborgir, then rejoin me here."

* * *

The álfar bowed and repeated the Veil-piercing ritual. They soon reappeared, though it felt like hours to Grýla.

She straightened her bowed back. "I need your aid to rescue my sons held by Krampus at the Rock of Dunamase."

"We know of an enchanted spot in the dungeon there," replied the tallest álfar with unearthly calm.

"I bid you take me," replied Grýla. "You hidden folk can move unseen to locate my sons. I shall break their shackles and then you can return us to Dimmuborgir."

Two álfar circled Grýla and the four passed through the Otherworld to a dank dungeon reeking with despair. The tallest álfar signaled Grýla to remain still. The álfar vanished.

The dawn arrives soon, thought Grýla, struggling not to race down the dark corridors calling for her brood.

Eventually, the álfar reappeared. "We found your eight sons. They appear to have been whipped and are chained to the wall of a large cavern."

Grýla's eyes narrowed. Her fists clenched of their own accord. "Take me there."

The álfar vanished. An invisible hand guided Grýla.

She crept with all the stealth an old troll can summon, cringing at the soft patter when her foot disturbed an unseen pebble. Sputtering torches periodically lit the stone passageways through a series of turnings that Grýla committed to memory.

At last, they passed through an archway, entering a high-vaulted cavern. Grýla's bloodied sons stood chained to the far wall, their arms shackled over their heads.

A low gasp escaped Grýla's mouth and she raced to her trolls, hope returning to their faces. Grýla enclosed her copper amulet within a wrinkled fist and muttered a spell.

The thick iron chains binding the trolls rusted and crumbled, as if five centuries passed in an instant. Her sons collapsed to the floor.

"Hurry," Grýla whispered, a solitary snail of a tear meandering down her leathery cheek. "I will treat your injuries later. First, we must escape. Follow as quietly as you can."

Her sons struggled to their feet and staggered after Grýla.

A booming voice brought the trolls up short. "Who do we have here?" said Krampus, bending his goat legs so that his horned head could pass under the archway. Thirteen black-cloaked witches filed into the cavern behind him. "Well, if it isn't Grýla."

Her shoulders fell. "Save yourselves," Grýla breathed to the álfar, knowing there was nothing the hidden folk could do for the trolls now. Her sons huddled behind her.

"I planned to make a stew of these eight trolls," said Krampus. "But I'm sure my cauldron can accommodate one more."

"I thought you only ate mannfólk," Grýla replied, her mind racing to find a way to save her sons.

"And so I did. But I have discovered the advantages of straying from the old ways," he added, gesturing toward his new witch allies.

I am lost, but at least I can save my sons, thought Grýla. Her face hardened. She yanked the copper amulet from her neck, snapping the fine chain. She began chanting, summoning the deep magic.

Krampus's eyes widened as he recognized a spell to conjure a lake of lava that would engulf the castle and all within. "You would destroy yourself *and* your sons?"

Grýla paused. "If I cannot save them, then I shall take you and your coven with us to Hel. Unless—"

"Ah. I'd hoped there was an unless," replied Krampus.

"If you let us go, I will snatch no more ill-behaved children. They are all yours, from now to the breaking of the world." *I will starve*, she thought. *But my sons will survive.*

"Hmmm. Far preferable to being consumed in fire. Will you *swear* to it?" Krampus asked, raising his eyebrows.

"I tell you three times," replied Grýla.

"I hear you three times," said Krampus, completing the ritual. He gestured toward the archway. "You may go."

The witches parted to make way for the trolls.

* * *

Home at Dimmuborgir, Grýla's sons honored her by preparing a celebration with the food stolen from Ireland.

Grýla eyed the banquet ravenously. *But the old ways...* she thought, the weight of her immense age pressing down upon her. She smelled good things to eat from far away across the world. Her empty belly rumbled.

"Try some sausage, Mother," pleaded Bjúgnakrækir. "Please."

She sighed. *I must change if I am to survive. And I swore a solemn oath.* Grýla took a tentative nibble. Her eyebrows rose and a fissure of a smile cracked her stony face. Like a loose pebble on a mountainside, the sausage triggered an avalanche of eating. An hour later, a thunderous belch echoed in the halls of Dimmuborgir, signaling the long overdue end to Grýla's fasting.

And from that day to this, Grýla never ate children again.

Author's Note

Krampus is described in Central European folklore as a chain-wielding half-goat, half-demon who swats misbehaving children with birch branches and kidnaps other children during the Christmas season. In some regions, he is considered a companion of Saint Nicholas.

This story contains seven references to *Where the Wild Things Are* as an homage to Maurice Sendak's trolls.

The castle names and Icelandic foods mentioned are authentic. Grýla, Leppalúði, and their thirteen troll sons (the Yule Lads) are widely known in Icelandic folklore. They're even featured on postage stamps. Grýla is reputed to kidnap and eat misbehaving children during Yuletide. Her sons commit oddly specific mischief in the thirteen days leading to Christmas:

Stekkjastaur (Sheep-Cote Clod)—His stiff peg legs impair his ability to catch and eat sheep.

Giljagaur (Gully Gawk)—He hides in gullies, awaiting opportunities to sneak into cowsheds and steal milk.

Stúfur (Stubby)—He's very short and steals pans to eat any leftover crumbs.

Þvörusleikir (Spoon-Licker)—As his name suggests, he steals and licks wooden spoons. But apparently, he's not good at it, for he is very thin.

Pottaskefill (Pot-Scraper)—He does to pots what Stúfur does to pans.

Askasleikir (Bowl-Licker)—He lurks under beds awaiting opportunities to steal food bowls.

Hurðaskellir (Door-Slammer)—He slams doors, particularly at night.

Skyrgámur (Skyr-Gobbler)—Skyr is Icelandic yogurt, and this fellow gobbles it down.

Bjúgnakrækir (Sausage-Swiper)—He lurks in rafters to swipe sausages being smoked.

Gluggagægir (Window-Peeper)—Restraining orders don't stop this troll from peering through windows in search of items to steal.

Gáttaþefur (Doorway Sniffer)—His large nose gives him an acute sense of smell with which he seeks laufabrauð (leaf bread).

Ketkrókur (Meat-Hook)—He uses a hook to steal meat. Not creepy at all.

Kertasníkir (Candle Beggar)—He steals candles from children and eats them (the candles, that is).

Blue Roses Grow in Salem

Jane Nightshade

"**B**lue roses! Unnatural coloration of God's beautiful creation. 'Tis witchcraft, plain and clear!" A coarse-voiced woman called from the crowd, which looked like a small inky sea of men and women draped in sober black, indigo, or gray. The men were unwigged and there was not a hint of real color in the garb of the women and girls, only the drab hues of Puritan respectability.

Amity didn't know the woman who shouted the crude charge, or most of the others in the crowd who jeered and spat at her. Commonwealth soldiers had dragged her from her home, a small freehold located between Salem Village and Salem Township, full of dust and stones and moldering chicken feathers. She'd lived alone since GrandPapa passed on a year and a half ago, and she didn't have much opportunity for socializing in town. The main joy of her life was her rose garden, now trampled and destroyed by angry villagers.

She mostly only knew Goodman Tarrant, the grocery man who bought her chicken and goose eggs for his market stall, and his two apprentices, the bonded servants Tom and Increase. Plus his tart-tongued, rawhide-skinned goodwife, Goody Tarrant—about whom the less said, the better—and the Tarrants' maidservant, Sarah Drew. "A young mistress alone is an affront to nature and God," Goody Tarrant once declared to her husband, not realizing that Amity was within hearing distance.

Now, most of the Salem townspeople, inflamed by rumors of witchcraft, seemed to agree with Goody Tarrant, who had been ailing the last Amity knew of her.

Another loud voice proclaimed, "A fair miss who lives alone, aye—a decent girl of eighteen years would be married."

"Old Miles Cleary, a strange one he was. I shouldn't doubt if it was he who learnt her to bewitch," another said.

Amity clenched her fists at her sides and felt red flames grow from her pale, petal-shaped cheeks. It was one thing if they mocked and slandered her own self, but quite another to lie about GrandPapa. Still, she held her tongue. Bewildered by her arrest at first, she was starting to feel a creeping awareness of high danger. "There's naught to be gained by answering them back," GrandPapa would have said.

It was GrandPapa who'd planted the famous Cleary rose garden—famous at least in Salem Village. Cuttings that he brought as a young man from England, all the way across the ocean, lovingly cared for during the long, perilous trip. He'd planted them on his land, and nurtured them for twenty years, his pride being the dainty white rose.

And now, from the confusing charges the Commonwealth guards had shouted as they arrested Amity, it appeared that Goody Tarrant had gone to her rest, and that the white rose was somehow considered a factor in her demise.

A soldier of the Commonwealth Guard—there was one at each elbow—prodded her to walk faster, as the crowd grew angrier and more restless. "Give way," the soldier said roughly, shoving a village man who tried to grab Amity. "'Tis a matter of the law—for Justice Hathorne!"

The village man spat at the ground. "The Devil's whore!" he yelled, and the crowd took up the chant. "Devil's whore! Devil's whore!"

The guardsmen shielded Amity from the crowd's view as best they could and hurried her along to the courthouse where the notorious Justice Hathorne presided. Amity's heart thundered at the thought of the fearsome magistrate's name. GrandPapa knew him long before he became a high court justice. She recalled GrandPapa's assessment of the man with rising anxiety: "Eye o' brimstone, crow's wings for eyebrows, dried lemon-skin in place of a mouth—that be John Hathorne! With a heart like a raw diamond and a hide of granite, cruel as a Maine winter. Unfeeling, unseeing, unhearing! There's devilry afoot in this land sure enough—but not the species of which he thinks there is!"

They paused at the door of the courthouse, just as Goodman Tarrant arrived at the same destination, flanked by several male supporters, and the maidservant, Mistress Drew, whom Amity favored with a faint nod. Sarah Drew was the closest she had to a friend in town. Goodman Tarrant gave Amity a hard blue eye and heaved an angry sigh. The crowd quieted and watched both of them, straining to hear any words exchanged.

Amity fought back the instinct to drop her own eyes under his withering stare. She'd done nothing wrong—why give Tarrant and the crowd the satisfaction of seeing her act as if she did? She met Goodman Tarrant's hard look squarely, gazing straight into his face with what GrandPapa called her "gray-green-lichen" eyes.

He spat at her feet and said, with cold and measured deliberation, "Get thee behind me, Satan."

"Satan has no purchase on these pitiful bones," she replied, clear and even in her voice.

"My, she's a brazen one, isn't she!" cried a coarse-looking woman from the crowd.

Goodman Tarrant said nothing more, but turned his back and entered the courthouse, along with his supporters and Mistress Drew. The latter lowered her eyes and blushed, avoiding Amity's gaze.

"'Tis a right comely lass, that one," mumbled someone, as the Tarrants' maidservant trudged through the courtroom's entrance. Sarah Drew, tall and yellow-haired, often reminded Amity of a goldenrod stalk. She didn't understand why Sarah had ignored her nod and avoided her gaze, but she knew it was not a good sign.

* * *

"Promise me, child, that you will tend the roses as your children," GrandPapa had said, as he sank into his deathbed. "The white rose, you must tend the most precious of all."

Amity had promised to obey his dying wish with fervent assurances. She'd cared for them as GrandPapa had taught her, pruning in the dead of winter, spraying the leaves with vinegar to keep out the mold when rain and damp came, watering daily in the summer. She followed GrandPapa's instructions even when cutting bouquets for the vases inside the gray, wooden-sided farmhouse with two gables that he'd left her—"Take where the leaves are joined in five, not three."

Now she was about to climb into the dock, to stand before the fearsome Justice Hathorne, the man who'd sent a near score of Salemites to their cruel deaths, accused of witchcraft.

Her crime: sharing a bouquet of her white roses with Goody Tarrant when she was ailing, and allegedly enchanting the roses so that the goodwife had died.

Someone nudged her gently from behind to the steps that led to the dock. Amity turned to see the Commonwealth guard who had pushed the threatening villager away from her out in the street. He whispered softly, "Cheer up, Mistress, 'tis only a hearing. It may be sorted out and there'll be no jury trial. It's juries you have to watch for—Hathorne can do nothing without a jury."

Amity startled. She realized for the first time that the guardsman was young, handsome, and kindly natured. He had tawny brown eyes with thick lashes, and a golden sheen to his skin.

She nodded and stepped up into the dock, fearful but hopeful at the guardsman's words. Perhaps it really was all a misunderstanding, and no jury trial would be called.

"Now Mistress Cleary," started Justice Hathorne, "how came you to make these wretched blooms turn *blue*? What enchantment has caused it?" He gestured toward a wilting bunch of once-white roses standing in a glass jar of water, perched in a prominent place on his imposing judge's bench.

Amity straightened her back and tried to keep the tremors out of her voice. "I cannot give an account for it, my lord justice."

Justice Hathorne was unmoved. "What evil spirit have you consorted with? Name the demon!"

"No one, my lord."

"Have you signed the Devil's book of promised souls?"

"I've signed no book, my lord."

The judge shook his head. The muscles in his face tightened with fury. "We shall call on the first witness for the providence of proof," he stated coldly, banging his gavel with an ominous thud. "This be the last chance for a confession for the salvation of your soul."

"I cannot sign for what I have not done, my lord. The Lord of Hosts suffers not the company of liars."

Justice Hathorne's black brows swooped downward, almost obscuring his sulfurous eyes. Amity remembered, with a shudder, how GrandPapa had likened his brows to the wings of crows—screeching birds that eat carrion. "Bailiff, you may summon the first witness."

Sarah Drew stood up from the gallery, where she had been sitting amongst her master, Goodman Tarrant, and his supporters. Amity watched fearfully as she made her way to the witness seat on the justice's left side, then swore her oath and sat down.

"Mistress Drew, kindly recount the events of the day before yesterday, concerning the accused woman's gift of flowers to Goodwife Tarrant."

Sarah stumbled at first but eventually gained strength and confidence in her comments. Newly arrived from England just two years before, she spoke in the accent of roughest London, though few in Salem would recognize that fact. They did, however, recognize her as foreign, not born in the colonies. Sarah had spoken to Amity several times about how much of an outlander she felt in Salem, and Amity had pitied her for it.

"S-s-h-eee...Mistress Cleary...drove into town to sell her eggs to my master, Goodman Tarrant. She had a bunch of white roses in her ox cart with the eggs."

"And what did she say to you, about the roses?"

"She said, 'I have heard news of Goody Tarrant's poor constitution. Take these for the cheering of her health.'"

"And what did you do with this bunch?"

"Set them in a vase with water, and then took them to Goody Tarrant, who was lying abed with the grippe."

"And Goodwife Tarrant? What be her constitution afterward?"

"Worse. She took worse, my lord! Not two hours later she pitched a fit and screamed in pain. She screamed on and off throughout the eve. I tended her as best I could, but by morning..." Here Sarah faltered and wiped a tear from a corner of her eye.

"Morning? What transpired in the morning? Speak up, girl!"

Sarah's eyes darted around the courtroom nervously. "Goody Tarrant was far gone to meet her reward, and she passed on to the Lord at nine o'clock on the morn."

"Was it your notion that Goody Tarrant was cursed by these flowers and expired because of it?"

"Not at first, my lord. 'Twas only when I saw what became of the..." here Sarah shuddered and put her hands over her face briefly, "those things! White blooms, all turned blue overnight! Sitting on Goody's washstand, blue as one would please. Then I knew, 'twas witchcraft what done poor Goody in."

There was a collective gasp and cry from the gallery box, and Amity drew back in shock. Her only real friend was her main accuser!

All eyes turned to Goodman Tarrant. He rose quickly, pointed to Amity, and called out, "This witch killed my poor Bess dead! Before her time! Heaven cries out for justice!"

Justice Hathorne banged his gavel. "Silence! I will have no more outbursts in this courtroom. Mistress Drew..." he turned to the blonde girl, "is it possible the blooms were dipped in some coloring agent, such as indigo dye?"

"No my lord. If they were dipped, the dye would have run off, for the surface is poor for taking it. And the petals might have shriveled from the harshness of the substance."

All eyes turned toward Goodman Tarrant and then to Amity, who had fainted dead away.

* * *

Amity woke up to find herself on a bed of moldy straw in a rough chamber of the Salem Village gaol. There was a dirt floor and one small paneless window barred with iron. The door was heavy oak reinforced with iron bands, with a small, barred opening at eye level.

"All these bars and stout oak for a simple girl like me," Amity said aloud.

She was lonely and cold, for all it was a soft evening in May. The heavy walls of the gaol kept the warmth out, save what wafted through the barred window. She piled straw under the window and stood on it, holding up her hands to the plain air coming through the bars, trying to get warm.

There was a loud knock on the oaken door. "Halloo there, Mistress. I've brought you some food." The voice sounded familiar.

She heard the clanking of a key and then the thick door opened to a man carrying a rough tin tray. Amity realized with amazement that it was the Commonwealth guardsman, his uniform blouse loosened and his helmet off.

He was more handsome than ever, with his tawny hair liberated from the helmet and tumbling to his shoulders. Amity reckoned he was about a year or two older than she was, with an enviably well-made form.

"You...you are my gaoler? When was it that Commonwealth soldiers became keepers of prisoners? Is that not the province of the gaoler?"

The guardsman laughed. "A tuppence or two to stout Constable Colvin and he kindly allowed me to deliver your dinner." The soldier offered the tin tray. Upon it was a single round of rough bread, a tin cup of water, and a small wedge of moldy cheese. "Surely you are famished. It's been hours since...since the arrest."

Amity regarded the tray with weary indifference. She knew it had been a long time since her last meal, but somehow hunger was the last thing from her mind. "I can scarcely look at it."

"Eat," commanded the guardsman. He made up a pile of straw into an impromptu tuffet. "I will sit here until I see you eat." He placed the tray at Amity's feet and sat on his pile.

"Why do you take an interest in me? I am nobody."

"Because you are innocent."

"How do you know it?"

"I know. The Higher Power knows. Now, eat."

"I do not know that God has even noticed my wretched soul."

"You've been noticed. Now, eat. And then, we talk."

The handsome man was so sure of himself, so kindly and concerned, that Amity felt a sense of ease for the first time since the guardsmen had come to White Rose Farm with a warrant for her arrest.

Obediently, she tore a piece off the round of bread and chewed it with vigor. It was stale, but not yet hard enough to be inedible. "So," she began, after swallowing a good portion of the bread, "what is it that you wish to speak of to me?"

"Your defense."

"I've not been allowed a barrister or any kind of advocate. And would not have coin to pay for such a thing, anyway."

"You have the right to question accusers. Even Justice Hathorne cannot deny it."

"But I have no knowledge of the law!"

"You won't need it, as long as you keep a cool head and follow the scheme I have wrenched together—to the letter."

"You speak in riddles, good soldier."

The guardsman leaned forward until his face was close to Amity's. Amity's heart began to beat faster. The soldier was not only very handsome but seemed to give off a radiant manner of force, an essence of being, that made him seem far above an ordinary man.

It occurred to her that she hadn't asked his name. She was just about to say something when he spoke.

"All will be clear, Mistress. First, you must start with Mistress Drew..."

"I don't understand Sarah's testimony. She knows me and knows that I couldn't wish harm on a horsefly."

"Just listen, Mistress."

Amity listened attentively for an hour or so, her heart quickening, until Constable Colvin rapped heavily on the oaken door and warned the soldier that his time was up. When he had gone, she realized that she still hadn't asked for his name.

She pulled her woolen broadcloth cloak around her and huddled on the pile of straw. Outside, the street was quiet, but for the sound of some kind of creature—an owl or perhaps a bat —beating its wings furiously against the bars of her single cell window. She remembered GrandPapa's words—"there is devilry afoot in this land, sure enough"—and she was afraid.

* * *

When two guardsmen came to escort Amity to the courthouse, she was disappointed to see that her tawny-haired soldier was not one of them.

The courtroom was full to overflowing. Amity approached the dock yet again with trepidation, as onlookers in the gallery jeered at her until they were silenced by the bailiff. She glanced around the room as she ascended the steps to the dock and spied a figure with a familiar stance in a far back corner. It was her guardsman, standing stone-faced with eyes fixed on the crowd in the gallery. He caught her eye and almost imperceptibly nodded. Feeling bolder, Amity took her place in the dock.

Judge Hathorne's eyebrows swooped down toward his eyes like black wings. "Mistress Cleary, are you inclined this morning to confess your consortion with the Master of Lies and beg for the salvation of your soul?"

"No, your Lordship. I'm in—in...*inclined* to claim my right to question my accusers."

The judge's brow swooped down even lower and more furiously. He summoned an officious-looking young man to the bench and conferred with him in whispers. In full voice he addressed the court. "I regret that the suspected witch must be allowed to address questions to her accuser, as is laid out under the Rights of Englishmen. Call your witness, Mistress," he said to Amity.

Amity squared her shoulders and descended from the dock. With a slight tremble in her voice, she approached the witness box and said loudly, "I call to the stand Mistress Drew. Mistress Sarah Drew."

The crowd in the gallery murmured as Sarah Drew ascended to the witness stand with downcast eyes. She blanched and struggled to meet Amity's gaze. Amity fought back any sense of empathy with her erstwhile friend. *It's her or me*, she thought, pulling herself up straighter.

"Mistress Drew," Amity began, "how long have you lived in Massachusetts Colony?"

"Two years this past February."

"And before that you lived in London, in the Mother Country, did you not?"

"Yes."

"What did you do to earn your keep in London?

"I kept a flower stall in Covent Garden, with my old Mam and Father."

Justice Hathorne banged his gavel. "Mistress Cleary," he said icily, "what has this line of interrogation to do with the charges at hand?"

"It speaks to the witness's knowledge in matters of a floral nature," replied Amity, with a coolness and self-assurance she did not feel.

The judge faltered uncharacteristically in his speech and seemed to have found himself unable to think of a reason why the questioning could not continue. "Very well," he said in a grudging tone.

Amity turned to Sarah again. "You learned how to arrange the flowers, to make a sumptuous display for their purchase?"

"Yes."

"And occasionally, did you have a special order from someone who wanted an arrangement of specific colors? Some of them unnatural? To match a gown or a set of draperies?"

Sarah took in her breath audibly and scanned the gallery. Amity turned slightly sideways to follow her gaze and saw that her eyes had found Goodman Tarrant. He returned her look with a hard stare. Amity thought he was struggling to hide his expression from the crowd in the gallery. A few onlookers saw the exchange of glances between Goodman Tarrant and Mistress Drew and murmured.

Amity surreptitiously caught the eye of her young guardsman standing in the corner. He nodded approval and she felt even more emboldened.

"Well, Mistress Drew?" commanded Hathorne. "Have you an answer to the inquiry?"

Sarah made a small but noticeable gulp. "Yes. We did have orders of that nature."

Amity continued her interrogation relentlessly. "And what did you do to your flowers to fulfill such an order? Did you have a way of coloring them?"

"We...we...dyed them."

The gallery's murmuring got much louder. Justice Hathorne gaveled their voices quiet. Amity thought he, too, seemed as if he were struggling with himself. His cruel but cunning face bore the look of a man who wanted to halt the proceeding, but who had realized that it was too late; the crowd had grasped the implications of Amity's line of questioning and was slowly turning against Sarah Drew.

If Amity was suspect for being an outsider and an unmarried girl of eighteen living alone, Sarah was doubly suspect as an outright foreigner with shallow roots in Massachusetts. And it wouldn't have done for the justice to land too heavily on the side of a foreigner against a trueborn daughter of the Massachusetts Colony, even one suspected of being a witch.

"Proceed, Mistress," the justice finally said, nodding at Amity.

Amity's heart surged with triumph—and relief. She had barely thought she could stand in the court and do what her soldier had advised, but now, here she was doing it, and succeeding. She was actually succeeding!

"You testified on the day before this that flowers can't be dipped in dye, is that not correct, Mistress Drew? You said the dye would run off, or it would wilt the blooms, did you not?"

Sarah Drew nodded weakly.

"You must speak your testimony, Mistress," Justice Hathorne instructed in a stern voice. "Remember that the Lord will account the lying tongue most harshly on the Day of Judgment."

"Yes," she finally spoke. She looked down at her lap, as if wishing she could melt through the floorboards of the courthouse like butter melting from a stove.

"Isn't there another way to dye flowers? To put dye in the water and put the severed stems in the dyed water? And then let nature's green arteries do the work of spreading the dye to the petals, thus changing their color?"

"Y—es."

"By your hand, is that not what was done to the white roses I gave to you for Goody Tarrant's cheer?"

Sarah began to cry. "Yes."

"But why?" cried Amity in an injured tone. "What was the purpose?"

"It wasn't my plan," Sarah burst out through now-hysterical crying. "It was Goodman Tarrant's notion! He knew I had a trick for turning flowers! I put them in water and put indigo powder in the water! At morn, the work was done, and they were pale blue."

"For what purpose?" Amity repeated.

"Because he...he...helped Goody Tarrant to her rest with a downy pillow and schemed to arouse suspicions of witchcraft to cover it!" At this, Sarah put her head in her hands and began to sob uncontrollably.

"It's a lie!" Goodman Tarrant stood up from his seat in the gallery, scarlet-faced and shaking with rage. "*This* girl is the witch! I mistakenly accused Mistress Cleary, but now I see that the true witch was in my own household! Get thee behind me, oh Satan's strumpet!"

Sarah raised her tear-stricken face. "He is the teller of lies, not I! I knew nothing until the deed was done. He said afterward there was no sin, as Goody was already fading. He wanted to make me his wife. An old wife traded for young!"

At this outburst, the gallery crowd erupted in shouts, foot stamping, and cries of "Murder! Foul murder!" Goodman Tarrant yelled curses and pleas of innocence at the top of his lungs.

Justice Hathorne gaveled for order with several loud bangs. "Continue, Mistress," he said to Amity.

"But you weren't opposed to the idea of becoming the next Goody Tarrant?" she asked Sarah.

Sarah looked down again. "I was not opposed to it if Goody went to her rest by God's hand, but I swear by Him, the Giver of Providence, I did not know beforehand of Goodman Tarrant's deviousness."

The gallery erupted again in cries and charges directed at Goodman Tarrant.

Amity nodded grimly, then looked over at her soldier in the corner and saw with surprise that he sported a broad grin. *He's enjoying the spectacle*, she thought. *I'm certainly not. Sarah was my only friend.* Then the soldier sobered up and resumed a solemn expression when he caught Amity's eye. *Perhaps I've misjudged him. He is likely just glad for the exposure of my innocence.*

Justice Hathorne stood up—flouting protocol—and smashed his gavel furiously on its saucer as he towered over his high bench. "Order!" he shouted over the din. "The Crown must have order! Cease this pandemonium at once. Bailiffs, apprehend Goodman Tarrant with utmost alacrity!"

Goodman Tarrant struggled wildly in the grasp of the bailiffs, who eventually dragged him out of the courtroom. His shouted claims of innocence could be heard in the street as he was marched to the gaol. Sarah, too, was escorted from the courthouse by another official, her fate as yet unknown.

When the gallery had quieted, Justice Hathorne sat down. Amity had stood limply in front of the bench throughout the last, wild proceedings of her hearing, unnoticed. She was at a loss for a notion of what to do, when suddenly Justice Hathorne addressed her. His fearsome eyes affixed themselves on hers and Amity felt weak in the legs, dreading that he would somehow still find a reason to try her for witchcraft.

He looked as if he were chewing tenpenny nails as he spat out the reluctant words. "Mistress Cleary, it appears that it was but base human violence and not blasphemous devilry that accounted for Goodwife Tarrant's sad demise. The Crown finds you innocent of all charges and bids you to take your leave as a freeborn citizen of Massachusetts."

The gallery crowd murmured its approval—the same people, Amity fleetingly thought, who had called her the Devil's whore only an hour past.

Amity clasped her hands together with relief. "Thank you, my lord," she managed to say. She gathered her skirts up and turned to leave, thinking that the one thing she needed was a bath. She longed for her old empty flour barrel at home, made waterproof with pitch, which she filled with warm water from the kitchen hearth and sometimes floated fragrant petals in, when the rose garden was in season. Except that GrandPapa's famous roses were gone now. The garden could be replanted, but it would never be the same again.

Somehow, she had to find someone who could drive her back to White Rose Farm—instinctively she sought the friendly, handsome face in the corner she had come to adore. But her tawny-haired soldier wasn't there anymore. His spot in the corner was empty, and she could not see him in the gallery crowd that was quickly emptying out. Her heart sank; she wondered if she would ever have a chance to speak with him again. He had likely saved her life. Even if her romantic fancies about him came to naught, she knew she did at least owe him thanks for her rescue.

In the end, it was Goodman Tarrant's bondsman, Increase, who drove her back to White Rose Farm in his groceryman's vegetable wagon. Increase noted with an ironic tinge in his voice that his master did not have any use for the wagon at present.

At home, Amity set about feeding her chickens and geese, who had gone hungry for two days and were squawking up a riot. She found GrandPapa's old hunting dog, Flashpoint, similarly deprived, out in the woods, tearing into a pheasant he had just caught.

When she restored as much order as she could to her vandalized farmstead, she set about the laborious process of drawing water from the well, starting a fire in the stone kitchen hearth and heating the water for her bath. The sky was darkening when she finally finished the task.

She set up the old flour barrel in front of the kitchen hearth and poured the heated water inside, then sank into it gratefully. It felt like heaven after the dismal filth of the Salem gaol. She wanted to burn her reeking cloak and gown, but realized she couldn't afford it, so she resolved to spend half the day on the morrow soaping and scrubbing them as well as she could.

The thing to do, Amity thought as she soaked in the water with her head leaning against the top of the barrel, *is to get married. I will always be under suspicion of the town busybodies whilst I live here alone.* And again, her mind filled with fancies of her soldier, whose name she didn't even know.

* * *

Someone was rapping on the front door and it woke Amity from a deep sleep. She'd fallen into a heavy drowse while soaking in the flour barrel. Now she was awake and aware that the once-warm bath water was cold, and a man's voice was calling outside for her, in between sessions of rapping. "Mistress Cleary! Mistress Cleary! I bid you open the door!"

Amity was startled. Who could it be? She hadn't heard horse's hooves on the pathway to the farmhouse. But she might have been asleep. The rapping sounded urgent. The last time she'd heard that urgent rapping, it was the Commonwealth guard coming to take her away to gaol. Was it another witchcraft charge? Amity shuddered at the thought. But the rapping continued, and she had to see what it was about. It could be a neighbor in need or a traveler in distress.

She climbed out of the barrel, shivering, and reached for her old flannel towel and dressing gown. The only light was the soft dim glow of embers from the hearth. She fumbled for a taper and lit it from the embers. Wrapped in her dressing gown, still shivering, she made her way to the front door and steeled herself to open it.

It was a guardsman, just as she had dreaded. But it was *her* guardsman! The soldier who had saved her life. In the light of her taper, his face looked more handsome than ever. "By your leave, Mistress, may I come in? 'Tis a long ride from town."

Amity hesitated. How the town gossips' tongues would clack if it was known that she had entertained a young man alone without a chaperone...and at night, even! But she trusted him wholly. He had saved her life and would never hurt her. Perhaps...she dared hope...perhaps he had even come a-courting?

"Please do come in. I'm afraid you have caught me in a shabby condition of dress. Will you sit down while I make myself more presentable?" She lit all the lamps in the front parlor and bade him to sit on the threadbare silk settee that GrandPapa had brought from England so many years before.

She carried her taper upstairs and lit a lamp in her bedroom. Choosing a gown and petticoat was not a hard choice, for she only had two sets of clothes. The first set lay near the hearth in the kitchen and the second set was in her cupboard. She dressed as quickly as possible and pushed her straggling, disheveled hair under a lace cap.

It will have to suffice, she told herself, then traipsed downstairs in as short of an amount of time as seemed decent. Oh, *her* soldier!

She saw that he had taken the liberty of laying a fresh fire in the stone hearth of the parlor. He stood in front of it, gloves discarded, warming his hands.

When she alighted from the stairs, he turned around and smiled broadly. His whole body seemed to glow with golden light, although Amity realized it was probably just a trick of the fire, fooling her eyes.

"A free woman is our Mistress Cleary, now! How do you get on now that you are no longer living in the shadows of the gallows? And that you bested that mocking fool Hathorne, who would not know a real witch if she was the laundress who washes his underdrawers?"

Amity shuddered, thinking of her narrow escape. "It's...it's beyond wondrous." She sat primly in the winged armchair close to the fire, opposite the settee. "Thank you for laying the fire. Shall I put tea on?"

He leaned against the mantelpiece in such a casual way that some would deem it insolent. It occurred to Amity that she still didn't know his name. *Her* soldier's name.

"I have not come for tea, Mistress. But if you require it, please proceed."

Amity excused herself and went to the kitchen. She put a small log and kindling on the glowing embers in the hearth and poked up a heartier fire. Then she filled a kettle from a pitcher of water on the kitchen table and put it on to boil. There was just enough loose tea in the stoneware jug to make a few cups, she saw with relief. But shopping for new supplies would not be amiss in the near future.

She returned to the parlor and the winged armchair. She had a question in her mind, and there was no other course but to come out with it. "Would it be too forward of me to ask your name? You are, after all, leaning against my late GrandMama's mantelpiece."

There was a great flash of fire as a log rolled forward and split. The flames roared briefly and lit her visitor from behind. His face turned dark as a glow framed his form, and it took on a strange, unpleasant expression, almost leering or mocking. And then it was gone in an instance and she was again looking at her comely, kind stranger.

He gave a little gentlemanly bow in her direction. "Not at all, Mistress. My name is Scratch. Corporal Nicholas Scratch. Some do call me Nick. Glad to make your acquaintance, Mistress Amity."

She felt awkward suddenly at his use of her Christian name, and very shy. He was like no man she had ever known, but then she had not known many men in her life. GrandPapa, Goodman Tarrant, Increase, and the casual laborers who helped her tend White Rose Farm—that was the short length and narrow breadth of her experience with men.

It occurred to her again that a question about all that had happened in the past two days was nagging her. "If it not be too forward, may I ask you a question about Mistress Drew, my good Corporal?"

Again, the little bow. "Please do."

"How is it you knew that she was a flower hawker in her previous life? How did you know the method with which she made the white roses turn blue?"

Corporal Scratch laughed softly. "The Higher Power knows all and sees all, Mistress."

"Higher power? Surely you jest, sir?" Amity's voice shook a little. Had her soldier taken leave of his senses? Believing like a madman that he could receive instructions directly from God?

He laughed again. "Yes, it is a pitiful little jape. Truth be told, a guardsman from Boston passed through last year, and he told me of Mistress Drew's family and their flower enterprise over a brew in the tavern across from the Tarrants' grocery stall. They are well-known in London."

"Ah." Amity felt a small thrill of relief. "Quite a happy coincidence—for me. And Sarah—what's to become of her?"

"She is under guard, awaiting a charge of at least perjury— and perhaps more. You grieve for her?"

"I wouldn't call it grief. Regret that she was willing to lie about me for what she wanted."

"Is it such a terrible thing to lie for what one wants?"

"Why, yes, it is! The very idea!" She gripped the arm of her chair in indignation. "But enough of her. I feel as if I owe you a debt that can never be repaid."

The corporal removed himself from the mantelpiece and approached Amity and the winged chair. He looked so tall and powerful as he bent over her still form. Strangely, she hadn't noticed his great hulking height before. It was as if he had grown four inches since she first came to know him.

"Oh, but there *is* something you can do to repay me," he said, smiling in that odd, leering expression she'd seen before, when he had given her his name. He reached into his weskit pocket and produced a small, bundled object. "You can sign my book...and, in doing so, offer me a trifling tribute that I would be fair pleased to accept," he said, laughing, undoing the bundle.

Amity shrank back into the winged chair, feeling a sudden chill. She remembered dizzily the voice of GrandPapa blaming—in a joking way—the mysterious illness of his favorite hunting dog on "Old Scratch" and "Old Nick"—both nicknames that the casual laborers used for the One of whose true appellation they feared to speak. She felt her head spin, sensing that she owed a debt of gratitude to the One, and he had come to collect...his trifling tribute.

Amity tried to summon her speech, but it would not come. The logs in the kitchen hearth crackled and hissed into her silence as the teakettle boiled over.

The House on Summit Avenue

Colleen Ennen

THIRTIETH

The girl is sitting as still and as careful as she can in the passenger side of her mother's car. The mother is wearing a new black dress, which is stiff and uncomfortable, and she looks as stiff and uncomfortable as the girl has ever seen her; she fidgets at the stoplight and clears her throat in the silent car. It is what the mother had called "the dead of winter," and even with the heat on as high as it will go, the girl's nose and fingertips are cold. The girl is holding in her lap a blue tin her mother had handed her, and she is careful not to let it tilt. She watches the white snow drift down from the grey sky. They are visiting their friends in the city again, and the girl is glad.

Before, the mother and the girl came often to the city and to the stately brick mansion they pull up to just as the snow lets up. It once belonged to some lumber baron, but has long since been parceled into three tall, narrow townhomes. The door furthest to the right is the door the mother and the girl approach, the one they have always approached. It has quicksilver windows and beds of blue foxglove flanking the entry and an old greenhouse in back with patinated boning and a long, scratched wooden workbench just visible through the sheen of glass.

Ana Maria—this is the girl's name—has always loved this old, magic house as if it were her friend. Her mother's friends are a roundish man and a very freckled woman; they live in the house. The man is shorter than her mother and his face is often pink.

Before, the round man would greet them at the door with a round smile and a round voice and invite them in for coffee and biscotti. On this day, though, a grey-faced man whom Ana Maria has never seen before answers when her mother knocks.

Inside, the hall is unusually dim and silent, muffled by quantities of drapes not pulled back from the windows and corners unlit by any lamps. A few tarnished green slices of light slant in from the far end of the hall—where the kitchen is—and wink with dust. The curved staircase rises, dark and spinal, above Ana Maria's head in uneven parallelograms.

"Now Ana Maria, you must promise me that you will be quiet, and that you will stay out of the way, and that you will not bother Mr. and Mrs. Fiore," her mother says, and she is kneeling carefully in her heels and pressed clothes, and she takes the blue tin which holds the tarta that she has baked, and she is placing a hand on Ana Maria's shoulder, which is a thing she does not usually do, and she is looking intently into Ana Maria's face.

"Yes, mother," Ana Maria says.

"Good girl," her mother says and tentatively pats Ana Maria's shoulder. She follows the thin grey man down the hall towards the kitchen where Ana Maria can hear the round man and the freckled woman.

Alone, Ana Maria slips off her new shoes of shiny patent leather and lines them up neatly next to the door. She pads silent-footed up the stairs, looking, as she always had before.

Ana Maria is eleven years, seven months, and twenty-two days old and she has not been allowed to visit her only friend in four months and eleven days. When she sees two blue eyes flashing between the banisters on the fourth floor, she grins wide.

FIRST

Ana Maria is sitting as still and as tidy as she can in the passenger side of her mother's car, which is big and seafoam green and finned and the most beautiful car Ana Maria has ever seen. Her mother is wearing her favorite yellow dress and has two daisies tucked into her chignon and is the most beautiful woman Ana Maria has ever seen; she drums her glossy pink fingernails on the steering wheel and she hums along with the radio. It is raining but also still bright outside— a "sun-shower," her mother had called it. Ana Maria is holding a bottle her mother has handed her labeled *Port*. She watches the many different people on the sidewalk with their raincoats all in different shades of black and grey and brown, walking in front of buildings all in shades of black and grey and brown. Ana Maria's raincoat is red and they are going into the city in her mother's beautiful car. Her mother has never before taken her into the city, but they are paying a visit to some friends of her mother's who have a daughter near Ana Maria's age; they are to become friends.

Ana Maria is seven years, four months, and eleven days old. She lives far east of the city, near to the river and to a town with her mother, father, younger brother, and older sister (Lucia, who is dead, and unlives in the earth on the hill behind the house). Ana Maria is homeschooled by her mother, who became nervous and old-fashioned after losing Lucia. She sees very few girls her age.

Because the trip takes several hours, by the time they reach the house on Summit, Ana Maria is famished. When a round-shaped man wearing a smile flings open the door, her stomach growls angrily before he is finished saying hello.

He laughs. "Well, come in then!" he says in a warm, round voice. "You have perfect timing, young lady, lunch is just served!"

The inside of the home looks like what Ana Maria—from many books, and from no experience—imagines a museum or estate might look like. It is warm and bright and all carved wood and high vertical lines; big windows with many squares and triangles of colored glass in red and blue and green color the sunshine that fills the room up. In the dining room, a freckled woman is placing a platter and a bowl on a long, linened table. A delicate-looking young girl sits in the chair facing the door.

"Come in!" the freckled woman says. "You must be Ana Maria. It's nice to meet you. I am Sofia, and you met Matteo. This is our Francesca. Say hello, darling."

The thin woman hugs the girl around her thin shoulders, and they pass a moment between them smiling lovingly at each other.

"Hello," Francesca says softly and no longer smiling but not yet frowning.

Francesca's eyes are the same foxglove-blue as the flower beds outside; they watch Ana Maria assessingly throughout the entire meal. Francesca's table manners are precise and correct and Ana Maria feels wrong-footed and so she tries to watch Francesca and copy her. Francesca does not speak again until they are out of the parents' reach, having been told to "go and play." Up three winding flights of stairs is Francesca's bedroom, which is sunny and matches her eyes and also the flower beds.

"Right," Francesca says, closing the door. "Well first of all, it's 'Frankie' not 'Francesca.' And I'm going to call you 'Ana,' because Ana Maria-ing all over the place is going to get *exhausting*."

SECOND

The round man answers the door and kisses her mother on the cheek and calls her "*lovely Valeria*" when they arrive. This is a thing which surprises Ana Maria, as her mother very particularly does not like to touch people, not even Ana Maria. The woman with the freckles is in the kitchen speaking very fast on the phone to someone; she waves a greeting when Ana Maria and mother enter. Frankie dashes in through the French doors at the back of the house and pulls Ana out by her wrist, talking fast and animatedly.

Ana learns many new games on her second visit, which lasts the whole day. Frankie teaches her Archaeologist, and they hunt for mummies and tombs in every hidey-hole of the house. Each time they scream, one of the mothers calls up "*Girls!*" which makes them giggle. Frankie shows Ana all the best spots for hiding, and the mice skeletons in the attic, and the dead baby bird in the chimney, and all the plants in the garden. Frankie teaches Ana about Bloody Mary and they chant her name into each mirror in the house. For a little while they spy on the adults in the sitting room where they have taken their shoes off and are sipping candy-red drinks from triangular glasses. But they are talking about dull things.

At dusk the girls run like wild things through the garden and try to catch fireflies in their hands until Frankie loses her breath and has to sit.

NINTH

Ana mentions Lucia while they are lying on the bed in the bedroom with the lavender wallpaper; Frankie demands an explanation. Frankie makes demands with the confidence of an only child much loved and never—as far as Ana has ever seen—scolded by her parents. Frankie is watching the crack in the ceiling for any ghosts which might come through from the *other side*; she declares it is a portal to the underworld. This is another of their games. Ana is listening to Frankie's cough rattling like change in your pocket.

"Maybe Lucia is a ghost," Frankie says.

"Maybe she's undead. A vampire. Or... something," Ana says. "And that's why mother spends so much time at her grave and has so many crosses."

"Wait! I think I hear a spirit," says Frankie. She shushes Ana, but they hear nothing. "I'm bored," says Frankie. "Let's do Murder instead."

Frankie and Ana have made many imagination games together. Their newest and favoritest is Murder. They are detectives investigating a ghastly homicide; there is always a lot of blood. They usually have to spy on the grown-ups to get clues. Sometimes Ana's mother and the man and the woman drink coffee or tea in the dining room and spend a lot of time staring at the walls and the ceiling and the floor and not saying much, and sometimes the freckled woman isn't there and her mother and the man drink wine together on the couch and say many things. These are not helpful clues for Murder.

FIFTEENTH
"What do you mean, you never had any friends before?" asks Frankie, then: "Hold still." She is daubing white face paint across Ana's cheekbone.

"I was only young when Lucia died," Ana says. "And after that, Mother didn't like to let me go places or do things. She teaches me at home." She opens her eyes to see Frankie frowning at her hands, which are shaking.

"So have you seen her ghost?" asks Frankie.

"I don't think so," says Ana, and then, "That might be nice, like always having someone to play with."

"Hmm," says Frankie. "And no friends in the neighborhood?"

"We live on a farm. There isn't really a neighborhood," says Ana, her face heated under the paint. "There's an old couple down the road and they give me sweets sometimes," she adds.

"All to myself then!" laughs Frankie. "Just the way I like it." She takes Ana's hands and lowers her back onto the bed of foxgloves they had gathered, twitching a few blooms into place here or there, assessing. "Okay, fold your arms over your chest like this. Now close your eyes and hold still and look dead," Frankie commands. She climbs up onto the stepstool with her camera, and looms over Ana for a long time before she takes her photograph. "Now we do me!" Frankie says, and jumps.

TWENTIETH

The hot summer afternoon is broken by a sudden rain shower which interrupts Frankie's and Ana's game of Dead And Buried, which is like Hide And Seek but the hider is a corpse and the seeker is a body snatcher. Ana had not known about body snatchers before Frankie taught her about them; Frankie knows a lot of things. The freckled woman is not there at the house that day to tell the girls to come inside at once; the round man and Ana's mother are there, but they do not call for the girls. The rain quickly soaks the girls and they give up their game to run in the wet grass with their bare feet, shrieking. When the rain on their skin becomes chilling, they dash into the old greenhouse and the air is still and sweet-green smelling and warm.

"Up here, what do you see?" Frankie says, and climbs onto the old table, which resembles a much-gouged antique surgery table. She is wheezing a little but does not mention it. Ana climbs up too and they lie on their backs and look through the glass roof at the clouds and at the skeletal dead oak branch hanging over them and at the willow tree branches whipping and whirling in the sudden wind.

"I don't see anything," Ana says. "Just loads of grey clouds."

"I see birds," Frankie says. "Lots of them. Swallows or crows or something."

They lie pressed side to side on the table. Frankie's bronze curls glow green-patinated in the leaf-filtered light; they coil into Ana's black hair, which absorbs the light hungrily. A spray of lightning lights up the greenhouse and Ana is looking at Frankie and she sees her for an instant bleached white and glowing in the light.

And then the skeleton branch crashes through the glass roof at one end with a great noise and sends a spray of glass and sparkling dust down on the floor and into the girls' hair. Ana cries out and tumbles from the table and Frankie does not cry out and sits up and looks out at the storm. She laughs and soon Ana laughs too. They laugh and eat plums they had stolen from a neighbor's garden earlier and the juices run down the sides of their faces and into the shells of their ears and into their hair and over their necks.

Their mouths are stained purple when they come back into the house at twilight when Frankie is supposed to. But Ana's mother and the round man are not in the kitchen or dining room or parlor and they cannot find them in any of the rooms on the first floor and Ana is at first frightened that they may have left, but when she runs to the front door, her mother's car is still there, and when she closes the front door and calls for her mother, she hears her mother call back *"Coming! Just a moment!"* from upstairs.

TWENTY-SIXTH

Frankie and Ana are not allowed to play outside anymore and not allowed to run. But the house is large enough for them to play in—with many bedrooms and bathrooms and cupboards—and they manage many of their favorite games like Murder and Dead And Buried, as well as playing Archaeologist and Witches and Ghost Hunters and Funeral. Funeral is their newest game. They take it in turns to deliver emotional eulogies about imaginary and fantastic lives they invent for the other, who lies still and careful in the cart of dumbwaiter until they are lowered to the basement while humming a grave funeral dirge.

When they sneak to the butler's pantry to spy on Ana's mother and the man and the woman for Murder, the three adults are sitting at the kitchen table, each on their own side, each bowed with scythe-shaped spines and drawn-bow shoulders, each staring at the tabletop, each gripping hard to stoneware mugs. None of them are speaking. The freckled woman may have been crying.

When night falls and Ana and her mother have still not left and the adults are speaking loudly now downstairs, Frankie and Ana climb into the deep windowsill in Frankie's bedroom, and prize the window open, and scoot half out onto the roof with their upper halves, and look at the stars and invent their own constellations and craft plans to fly away together from that very window into the night sky. All they have to do is jump.

"When I grow up, maybe I want to be an archaeologist or a journalist, and travel all over the world and see wild places and discover things and write about them," says Ana. "That didn't used to be what I wanted, but I don't think I want what I used to want anymore."

"I don't ever want to leave here, not even if I grow up," says Frankie, and this surprises Ana, who looks at her friend and sees a much more serious face than usual.

When Frankie begins to shiver, Ana helps her in and closes the window and uses a marker to map their new constellations in the freckles on Frankie's arm while Frankie repeats the stories they had invented for them so that Ana and Frankie can be sure they will remember.

THIRTIETH (CONT.)

"Ana!" Frankie hisses from between the banister railings on the fourth floor.

Ana's mouth stretches into a grin, and she trips the rest of the way up the stairs. "Frankie!" she whispers, throwing her arms around her friend's bony shoulders and burying her face in her cool neck. "T'so good to see you. M'glad you're better."

Frankie pats Ana's forearm with a cool hand but says nothing. Ana draws back and looks at Frankie properly. Her eyes and hair are paler and duller than they had been, as if a bit has been taken away, and she has dark purple-grey smudges beneath each eye, but she is there. She is there and Ana is glad. Frankie softly shushes Ana but takes her hand and turns to press her forehead to the space between the banister rails and peers at the hall below and listens intently.

Ana shuffles closer to try as well, but she can hear very little—only muffled voices, quite faint. She turns her head to look at Frankie again and sees her eyebrows are drawn down very low and her mouth is very flat and grim. She has never seen this expression before. From below there is a crash, and then several raised voices, and then a noise like a man crying. The sound makes Ana's stomach feel peculiar and she doesn't know what she is supposed to say. Frankie and Ana turn to sit with their backs to the rails, and hold hands in silence for several minutes until Ana Maria's mother softly calls "*Ana Maria*" and stands half in and half out of the front door.

"I'll be back," Ana says.

"I know you will," Frankie replies.

"Everything is going to be alright," Ana says.

"I know it will," Frankie replies.

Ana cannot read the expression on her face, but she squeezes Frankie's hand one more time and then slips down the stairs.

THIRTY-SECOND

Frankie isn't in the hall or her room this time, but Ana finds her in the attic. Her hair is tied tightly back and more of her seems to be missing. Her eyes are fully grey now, and her hair is silvery in the faint light. Ana's chest twists with worry, but then Frankie turns to her, and smiles her twinkling smile, and all is right again. They find old roller skates and glide back and forth across the attic, weaving around luggage and never-unpacked boxes. They ride the dumbwaiter up and down from the basement to the attic, together this time. They trace the still-faintly visible constellations Ana had drawn on Frankie's arm and repeat the stories. More than an hour passes this way.

Frankie freezes in the middle of a furious round of Miss Mary Mack and cocks her head. Ana can't hear anything for several minutes, but then she moves to the door and can hear them too. The adults are shouting downstairs. She makes out a few words, and thinks she hears "*Francesca*" a few times and also the words "*Get Out!*" Ana turns to look at Frankie, but Frankie is intently arranging the collection of blown glass paperweights on her dresser and pretending not to hear. She is wearing the same dress as last time, and the time before, Ana notices. A moment later Ana's mother calls for her to come, and Ana Maria goes.

THIRTY-FOURTH

Her mother has not brought Ana Maria to the house on Summit in three months, though sometimes when Father was away for work, she would tell Ana Maria to watch her little brother for a "*little while*" and would leave their home and go places she did not tell Ana Maria about, and Ana Maria suspects she might have been going to the city, but she knows better than to ask, even if her mother had never left Ana Maria and her brother alone Before.

Ana Maria does not think that her mother wants to be going to the house again, but she has been longing to go and finally they are going and so she does not ask questions about this either.

This time when Ana Maria and her mother arrive at the house, the round man and the freckled woman both meet Ana Maria at the door and say many nice things to her and each place a hand on one of her shoulders and lead her back to the dining room where they have laid out lunch. Her mother follows behind. The roundish man offers Ana Maria all sorts of food, and any kind of drink she could want, and the woman with the freckles sits very close to Ana Maria and asks her many questions about her studies and hobbies. Ana Maria's mother is silent and none of the adults are shouting this time. The man and the woman both watch Ana Maria with hunger eyes, deep pit black hole eyes, and even though she wants to go upstairs to see Frankie and to get away from their eyes more than anything, her mother gives her a look and she eats the sandwich the man made for her and the orange the woman peeled for her and the cake they both encouraged her to have. And then finally her mother tells her to go work on her homework and she can slide off of her chair and slip towards the door to the hall, but not before the man and the woman both hug her and pat her hair and sigh. When they release her, she darts to the stairs.

She bursts into Frankie's room and the girls throw their arms around each other and squeal as quietly as they can. And then Frankie leads her in a quick jig around the room that leaves Ana breathless and grinning, and Frankie laughing and twirling.

"I missed you!" laughs Frankie. "Where have you been?"

"Home," says Ana, still catching her wind.

"But why haven't you been to visit in *months*," presses Frankie.

"Mother," Ana says, and shrugs.

"Ineffable," says Frankie. And then she grins crookedly and twirls some more.

"You're so much better!" Ana says.

"Almost completely," says Frankie. "Soon it'll be just like before again."

Frankie declares that they "*absolutely have to*" play each of their favorite games that day, and they spend the rest of the morning running and hiding and ducking and jumping and laughing across the upper three levels, and the whole time Frankie doesn't have to stop to catch her breath even once. When it starts to get dark outside, they put on Frankie's favorite album and dance around her room to the Ronettes and laugh and forget to worry about how much noise they may be making.

"Francesca? Francesca?! Francesca!!" the girls hear the freckled woman call from outside Frankie's room, and she sounds frantic and confused but Frankie doesn't answer.

"Frankie, your mom is calling you," Ana says.

Frankie continues dancing.

"Frankie, she sounds upset," Ana says.

Frankie only stares at Ana and says nothing.

The freckled woman bursts through the door and looks around wildly and then sinks onto Frankie's bed and begins to weep and Ana does not understand. And then Ana Maria's mother is in the door and her lips are thin and white; she is shaking she is so mad.

"What. On Earth. Are You Doing. In Here?" her mother bites out between clenched teeth. She grabs Ana Maria's elbow and pulls her roughly from the room, hissing, "What is wrong with you?"

"I was just playing with Frankie!" protests Ana Maria, and the freckled woman wails and her mother's grip on her arm tightens. She yanks Ana Maria out the front door without stopping to grab their coats.

THIRTY-FIFTH

This time it is only one month until Ana Maria's mother brings her back to the house. It is also the last time her mother will bring her to the house, and the only reason they have come is because it has been explained to Ana Maria— repeatedly, at length and volume—that she needs to apologize to the man and the woman for upsetting them and for being "*ghoulish*" and for her "*disrespect.*" Ana Maria's mother was very clear that Ana Maria was not going there to play or to be petted and given treats or to do anything nice really—she was going to apologize and then they were going to "*close the book,*" though what book Ana Maria did not know.

And so, even though Ana Maria is still unclear what she is apologizing *for*, as soon as the round man admits Ana Maria and her mother to the foyer she stands as straight as she can and remembers the lines her mother repeated to her on the ride there: "Mr. Fiore and Mrs. Fiore, I am very sorry for my behavior the last time we visited. It was inappropriate and I should not have been in Francesca's room. I never meant to cause you any distress," recited Ana Maria.

She looks to her mother to see if she got it right and her mother nods, once. But the man and the woman are protesting that "*of course you have nothing to apologize for, dear,*" and "*we know how much you and Frankie adored each other,*" and many other things that confuse Ana Maria. Finally, her mother tells her to go play quietly in the front yard while she has "*a conversation*" with the man and the woman, and she gives Ana Maria a sharp little nudge when she looks longingly at the stairs up to the second floor. So, Ana Maria goes outside and sits on the front steps, between the twin beds of foxgloves, and sighs.

"Where have you *been*?" hisses Frankie in her ear, and Ana is so startled she tumbles sideways off the step. Lying in the dirt, in the shade between the plants and the brick front of the house, Ana looks up at Frankie's face looming over her upside down and she begins to smile.

"I—" she starts to say.

"Nevermind. We don't have much time," Frankie says urgently, and pulls her to a sitting position, still hidden from the street behind the blue and purple blooms. "I need your help."

"Anything," Ana says immediately.

"Good. I have a plan. I've been working on it slowly these past few months, but the timeline has changed," says Frankie while she crawls around the side of the house towards the back, jerking her head for Ana to follow.

"What plan?" asks Ana. "What timeline?"

They are creeping as stealthily as they can towards the greenhouse.

"They're selling the house," Frankie says and Ana is so surprised she stands straight up from her crouch in the middle of the backyard.

"What!" she yells, her brain buzzing.

"Shhh! You idiot, get down!" hisses Frankie. She pulls Ana right over by the ankles, and presses her into the ground with her whole body while she scans the house for any sign of movement. "Come on," she says when she is finally convinced that they haven't been spotted.

Ana meekly follows Frankie as they army crawl to the greenhouse, all the while growing more and more panicked. Her thoughts race and she thinks about the house and its parallelogram stairs and its beautiful patinated light and all of their secret spots and all of their games, which seem to be so much a part of the house's specific magic that they are unlikely to survive outside of it, and she feels tears stinging her eyes. Everything is changing and Ana hates it so much she feels nauseated. The house on Summit is going and Frankie will go too and she is starting at a proper school soon, her mother has just told her, and her parents are fighting and Father is sleeping in his office in the barn and—

"Quit blubbering," whispers Frankie.

And so Ana holds her breath to stop.

Once inside the greenhouse, Frankie stands and brushes herself off. Ana stands just inside the door and watches her bustle efficiently about the space, pulling boxes and bottles and bags of mysterious implements out from corners and piles and hidey-holes. She gathers her supplies on the big wooden workbench and mutters to herself all the while. Ana watches and waits and looks around at the unfixed roof and the swirls of leaves and dirt that have sifted in and settled on the floor and equipment and all the tables and benches, save the one in front of her with Frankie's pile of stuff. The greenhouse smells different; it's not green and alive anymore—everything smells like dust and petrichor and has an entirely new patina of earth and decay.

Ana gathers herself and calms her thoughts and takes a deep breath. "Okay, explain," she says.

Frankie paces a wide circle around the greenhouse with an intent look on her face. She makes one full circuit and then a second and then a third. A few times she pauses and opens her mouth like she is about to begin speaking and then closes it and resumes prowling.

Ana waits.

Frankie stops abruptly right at the point in her fourth orbit that is directly in front of Ana and turns to face her. "The thing is, Ana," Frankie begins and then stops, and looks closely at Ana, like she is looking for something in Ana's face but Ana doesn't know what. "The thing is," Frankie begins again, and then breaks off with a sigh. She combs her fingers through her hair and looks frustrated and then stomps her foot. "Damn—no, don't make that face, Ana, and stop being such a baby, *damn damn damn*—okay? Well, the damn thing is that nothing is the same. Not since it happened. And they want to sell the house and move—I don't know where they think they're going to move. Because they're sad and because they miss me, and the thing is *I miss them too*," she gets out finally.

"What are you talking about?" asks Ana.

"Parents and kids. Kids and parents. They go together like... something that goes together," Frankie says, distracted. "Even when they can be annoying sometimes."

"What? Frankie? What? They're just inside. Just go talk to them," Ana says, getting frustrated herself.

"I can't reach them," Frankie says, with an air of finality. "Not now. Not this way."

A creeping feeling of *something*—intuition or fear or worry or hope or relief or horror or all those at once—is stealing across Ana's back and shoulders and neck. She thinks everything is about to make complete sense and yet somehow no sense whatsoever.

"I don't know why I can't reach them, or why they can't reach me, but *you* can," Frankie continues.

"Frankie," Ana says softly.

"It's time for you to stop pretending you don't know," says Frankie, with uncharacteristic gentleness. She steps forward and places her hand on Ana's where it rests on the workbench and for a moment Ana feels the pressure of it and the coolness—odd coolness, she thinks distantly—on her skin, and then Frankie's hand sinks directly through her own and through the workbench and out underneath like it's less than smoke.

Ana tenses and freezes for several long moments. She resists the knowledge. In quick succession she flips through realization, denial, anger, grief, more denial, and finally— finally—she settles. She had known even if she had refused to know. There had been the snatches of overheard phone conversations and coded conversations between her parents over the dinner table about whether she should go or stay home, and receipts for flowers and the new black dress. There had been the man and the woman and their pain and their wasting away, and there had been the way that Frankie had changed and removed too. She just didn't want to know because Frankie was still *there* for her, and if she was still there everything was okay and would remain okay. But—

Now, maybe fewer things would need to change after all. Ever. Ana relaxes her shoulders and lets out a breath and pulls herself up onto the workbench cross-legged and looks calmly into Frankie's face and nods.

Frankie looks relieved. She nods back.

"What do you need?" Ana asks, and her voice sounds firm and Frankie-like in her ears.

"I need you to do something for me, Ana. Something important," Frankie says and steps closer, her eyes fixed intently on Ana. "Will you help me?"

"Of course," says Ana. "Anything."

"Are you willing to do what I ask—even if it's hard? Even if it's a little wicked?" asks Frankie.

"Anything," says Ana.

Frankie smiles. There is a foxglove stem in her hand.

THIRTY-SIXTH

The only time Father brings Ana Maria to the house on Summit, they are meeting Detective Carter there and everything is different. It has only been five weeks since she was there with her mother. Ana Maria is precisely twelve years old, but her father seems to have forgotten about her birthday and her mother is not at home to celebrate.

"Now Ana, I want you to think," says Detective Carter, as he crouches down to meet her eyes in the foyer. The house is empty and still, with sheets draped over most of the furniture. Father's hand is heavy on her shoulder, and Ana Maria notices he isn't wearing his wedding ring on it. "Try to remember everything you can about that day—the second. You and your mother came here together in the car—what color was your mother's car?"

"Seafoam," says Ana Maria. "Like the ocean."

"Good, yes. And you got here in the morning, do you remember what time?" asks Detective Carter.

"I think it was a little bit after ten?" says Ana Maria.

"Yes it was, good girl," says Detective Carter. "Now, what was the first thing your mother did when she came in the house?"

"I, I don't—" Ana Maria looks up at Father, but his face is closed and angry, with his mouth turned down and his eyebrow drawn in. "I think she took off her coat? Mr. Fiore took her coat and hung it there on the coat rack."

"Good. Okay. So Mr. Fiore greeted you at the door. Did Mrs. Fiore come to the door?" asks Detective Carter.

"Yes. I had to apologize and she came into the foyer and I did," says Ana Maria. She grips her gloves hard in her coat pockets.

"Now, think hard, sweetheart," Detective Carter says, and she doesn't like that—the "sweetheart" or his tone—but she can't say that to a police officer. "How did Mr. and Mrs. Fiore seem that morning when you saw them? Did they seem sick or tired or anything like that?"

Ana Maria squeezes her eyes shut and thinks hard. She sees on the inside of her eyelids the figures of the round man and the freckled woman and how he had seemed less round and how her freckles had looked like they were fading. She sees how they hunched over cups and saucers held in limp hands in the dining room and how her mother sat across from them in the chair, leaning towards them in a sympathetic angle and looking imploring. She sees Frankie standing gravely and a little blurry and strangely patinated behind them with a hand on each of their shoulders. "*Don't just stand there, bring us another pot of tea, Ana Maria,*" her mother had said.

"Maybe a little," Ana Maria says. "The man—Mr. Fiore—he was thinner and Mrs. Fiore was very pale, kind of grey? In the face?"

"Did they say anything about not being well?" asks Detective Carter.

"No, but I was outside for most of the time," she says. "After I apologized," she adds.

"Your mother left you outside?"

"No—well, she told me to stay in front so she could talk to the Fiores. She said it would only be a little while," says Ana Maria. She wants to get out from under the weight of her father's hand. She wants to leave the foyer and go looking.

"And was it only a little while?"

"No it was... we were there a while. I think it took longer than she thought."

"How long was your mother inside without you?" asks Detective Carter. He stands with a small wince and moves over to the stairs and sits down on the third step and pats the space next to him invitingly. Ana Maria moves towards the stairs because it seems like he wants her to but she does not sit down.

"I came in, I think I came in and it was a little before noon? I remember the grandfather clock chimed."

"What were they doing, the Fiores and your mother?"

"Having tea."

"Where was that?"

"In the dining room," she says and points down the hall.

The detective opens a small notebook and writes something Ana Maria cannot see on a fresh page. "In here?" he asks, as he stands and heads back into the dark, unlit house towards the dining room. Once inside, he feels for and then flips a switch and the electric lights are blinding to Ana Maria for a moment.

"Yes," she says, blinking. She thinks she sees a flicker of movement in the corner of her eye: the back hall.

"Now, this is very important: what did your mother do while they had tea? Did you see her make the tea? Or serve it? What was she saying to Mr. and Mrs. Fiore?" asks Detective Carter.

"I don't—I can't—I'm sorry." She begins to cry.

Detective Carter inhales carefully, and breathes out.

"That's okay," he says, "take your time."

Her father moves away from her and begins to pace.

Ana Maria wants to tell the detective that her mother didn't do anything, that she hadn't made the tea and that she hadn't cut the foxglove and that Ana hadn't even known what they were and that only Frankie had known those things.

But silhouetted by the French doors is Frankie, and she is holding a finger to her lips and looking very hard and very fierce at Ana Maria, and Ana Maria is frightened of Frankie for the first time in her life. Ana Maria nods slightly, just once, and Frankie smiles close-mouthed and flits back towards the greenhouse, golden and shimmering in the sun.

Proving Up

Caren Gussoff Sumption

O n a post in the gravel of the Upper Hoh's banks, my pink claim sheet swelled with moisture like a fat lip. It was right where the claim office promised, the first good sign of the last two days, if you didn't count the teenage four point buck staring me down like he knew something about me. His presence meant that there were still deer and elk running on the land—long-term sustainability, the Land Office described them—but I used the last of my resolve to stamp the ground and shoo him away. Once that resolve was used up, the last two miles were fueled by autonomics, the need to survive, and a soft-burning frustration that I wasn't allowed to ride my supply cart to the claim.

I could have kissed the sheet when I saw it. But I didn't. I unrolled it to double-check—there it was, "Puja Stevens, Claim #2371." My wrist GPS showed the supply cart ambling in, on schedule.

I was there. I could see a roof less than a hundred yards away. So, I did what that buck seemed to think I'd do: I broke down and cried.

The cabin was originally built in 1864, and had been renovated six times since. The last major rebuild was about forty years ago as a weekend retreat for some Seattle family of leisure, so, while it wasn't quite turnkey, it hadn't quite fallen down either. The door had flapped open at some point, and something had lived, mated, and died there—long enough that there was only the smell of mold, not death, but recent enough to have left dried remains.

I kicked the husk outside and unrolled my sleeping bag across the wooden floor. Moisture made the hardwood feel soft and fuzzy as fabric. A fire would dry it out, and the bleach on the cart would kill the patches of spores on the ceiling and walls.

But the trek made me too tired. I slipped in my bag and silently listed the orders of business: gather wood, make a fire, deal with the vial in my pocket, wait on the cart, and start my claim.

But later. Later.

For now, I could lie down, close my eyes, and rest. For now.

I was home.

* * *

Evalene Freeman kneaded her soft inch of belly fat, a nervous habit picked up after tossing her corsets into the fire her first week on the homestead. She'd saved the good spring steel from them, of course—she had not made it this far without a sense of thrift—and she was not sorry to see them go for other reasons besides the fact that it was far easier to wield a scythe against tall grass unbound.

Evalene was waiting for word from the office about the land, her land, this land, land claimed by Edward and rightfully hers, paid and filed and proved up into the only productive hay farm on the Upper or Lower Hoh.

But she knew if she prevailed, it wouldn't be because she built this farm mostly alone. Thom and Mary pitched in, of course, as their little arms were able. And Edward too, much as he could. Jonathan Bonner had helped her fell trees the first winter for the cabin and to clear the land. But Bonner had done it for a handshake agreement for future hay interests, which she had paid many times over, and never even hinted his want over the land until he went and filed this grievance.

If she succeeded, it wouldn't be that growing and harvesting hay in a rain forest demonstrated God's favor. It wouldn't be she'd exceeded requirements, or how she could quote their laws right back at them: that neither will or verdict can take a widow off a patent claim filed legally for government surveyed land, that Edward's Army service deducted from the length of residency obligated—even though they'd long surpassed that tenancy—and their cabin outdid the square footage needed by a neat ten feet on all sides.

No. She'd triumph because she told the Land Office in the plainest language of which she was capable she would dig Edward up and bring him right into their office to prove the Freeman claim, if they wished to disturb the mortal remains of a war hero.

And she would too. This was Freeman land now, Freeman land to lie in and pass along, even if Edward never set live eyes on it.

Evalene walked her fingers up and down her soft inch of flesh. She was never good at waiting. Not when she was a little girl, and certainly not as a grown woman. But then the wind started, gentle but bitter cold.

"What needs doing today, Bean-a-line?" the wind asked her. Edward called her that after their very first walk alone together, saying she was darling as a bean. Evalene couldn't see him yet, but the air around her brushed her cheek.

She didn't want to worry Edward just yet, and it was a fine enough day around it all, the children good at their letters books all morning. Thom could now read near as well as she could, and Mary was clever with her hands. Evalene thought about her children; she could not ask for more blessings, truly, even with outstanding legal issues and a dead husband. She decided to put away the worry.

"Fishing, I think," she answered. Edward and the children always loved fishing, though to Evalene it still felt much like waiting. But she could at least watch Thom and Mary scramble around in the air and sunshine, and feel the wisps of her husband's pleasure in the breeze as she held the pole.

Besides, they could see the cabin from the good bend in the river in case the land men did come. "I will get the children."

* * *

I couldn't tell how long I'd slept. It could have been minutes or hours, but with how cold and dead my feet felt and the close proximity of the cart, it must have been hours.

I checked my pocket, and squeezed my fingers around the vial before standing up and stamping the ground for the second time that day.

When the cart arrived—it looked like it'd show up this evening—I'd swallow the first of what would probably be a long string of sodium painkillers. Nothing beyond the standard issue, like my pack, sleeping bag, and satellite radio: noodles and soy, coffee, medicine and booze, even some cigs, both tobacco and weed. I used some savings to add a few flat stacks of pop-together furniture, solar lights, and basic tools.

When the cart arrived, I wouldn't have a thing to worry about except finding wood and Paulo's ashes.

And getting started.

Once, the land around the cabin had been cleared; there was even the ruin of what had been a barn. But now, the trees wove together a dense fabric of bushy undergrowth, wads of roots, draped heavily with licorice ferns and furry club moss. Dots and thin rays of sunshine penetrated through; overall, it was dark and rich, the air wet and thick with oxygen and dirt, fragrant as coffee grounds.

Getting wood was easy. Every tree in the wood stood ringed with a pubis of fallen branches. I didn't even need to cut; I could break them over my knee. I even had energy left to gather a few pounds of gravel from the riverbanks to line the wood stove, which would help the damp wood catch, then threw on some pitchy fir branches for a nice, quick flame.

The cart arrived at nightfall. Everything looked intact, including its battery. I tore open the medicine case and swallowed down two painkillers.

They worked quickly, and I felt strong enough to unload. What had seemed a lifetime supply came down to no more than twenty crates. They would have filled our room in the city, but here, they were troublingly diminutive.

The nighttime was louder than the day, and I could, academically, identify the forest and animal sounds: the hoot of an owl, or perhaps a sooty grouse; the delicate shamble of something fox-sized; a wailing coyote far in the distance and a wren warbling an answer. It seemed I used up all my sleep with my nap, so I listened until I was sure none of the sounds were anything to fear, then stood up, cranked on a kinetic flashlight, and padded around the cabin. My cabin. My home.

From the porch, the land was black but the sky was alight, more stars in one sky than the sum total of all I'd ever seen before. The stars made it easy to think about being without Paulo rather than just being alone on the homestead.

The homestead was his idea, his solution, to get out and away, live clean and free and healthy. He got us married so we could double the claim, placed us on the waiting list and enrolled us in the industry and vocation classes.

And Paulo talked once or twice about how we'd see the stars like this. In my mind, as I stood there and looked at the thousands upon thousands of tiny bursts, the times he mentioned that seemed to multiply in frequency and intensity.

I tried to look at the sky for both of us, looking up so high I couldn't help but open my mouth. "There they are," I said, like I would have said to him.

A twig snapped in a sudden wind. I was no longer alone.

I stood still to listen, holding my breath. It was a person, not a deer or elk or fox or bird. Someone was watching me, but when I tried to see who, all I could see was the pattern of a billion stars burned into my eyes, echoed across the black screen of trees. "Hello?" I called.

There was no answer.

"I have a gun," I lied, pulling my empty hands into my sleeves. "You're trespassing."

Still no answer. Still I was watched.

A small whirl of wind passed by me, a discernible cylinder about six feet high, smoky against the darkness, and very cold. I'd read about these, "devils" as they were called, when warmer air smacked into a pocket of colder air above it.

The devil blew past me. But, it spoke. It asked a question. Clear as the hoot and trill and howls outside. "Who are you?" it asked.

It was a very good question. Good enough to answer, even though I still couldn't see the asker and my hands, inside my sleeves, shook a little.

"Not sure," I said.

* * *

No word arrived by suppertime, so Evalene had Thom scale the fish and let Mary help her fry them in a little bacon grease.

It was always a pleasure to have too much to eat, as well as be able to go and leave some of the best parts for Edward on his grave. Evalene was not sure he could taste it, and she never wanted to waste time asking. He seemed so happy whenever she left him something that it did not really matter.

She made a pile of the fish straight on his mound, along with a rolled cigarette—from bags Evalene continued to have sent from the tobacconist Edward had long frequented—then sat down and waited for her husband.

She could not put off telling him any longer.

"My Bean, such a beautiful meal. And smoke." The air rushed around her, an embrace.

"I hope you enjoy it," Evalene said, as she held the rolled tobacco to pick at loose dirt. She pushed the fish into the ground like she was planting seeds, then replaced the cigarette across the grave neatly.

Edward would ask her to light it, to blow the smoke to him, since he could no longer hold it himself. She'd always abhorred the taste, the smell of tobacco, but had come to like it simply because, given the right amount from her lungs and a good angle, the smoke would frame Edward's features for a second. For a second, she could see his features, although blurry, like seeing his face through a pane of ice.

But it was his face.

"There is something bothering you. I could tell it yesterday." The cold wind blew under her chin, forcing her to look up. "You would never willingly volunteer to fish."

Evalene smiled a bit at that; nothing quite felt as good as having someone else know you as well as that. Then she laid her palm on Edward's grave. "Jonathan Bonner has given an affidavit that we have not satisfied the law," she said. "He claims he has done the proving up for this land."

The air turned hazy, grey. "We have paid him his due for his help the first year."

"We have overpaid him. Now he wants the homestead," she said. "I am waiting on a response from the land office."

Edward raised himself to his full height. He always cut an impressive figure: just over six feet with a barrel chest and a trim waist. His uniform had hung so well on him; sack suits never accentuated him as well as his formal wool frock coat did. That was how Evalene envisioned him in the pilaster of air: not the Edward she first met, a sweet schoolboy on the verge of manhood; not the gentle Edward she married, pine green eyes open during the kiss that sealed them; but this Edward, as she'd only seen him in his coffin, smelling of metal and wood-tar preservatives instead of his usual tobacco, dashing in navy wool, saber at his side.

The air spun, picking up dirt she had picked loose to bury the fish. "What did you tell the land office?" Edward asked through the wind.

"I told them everything," Evalene answered. She looked into the funnel. "Then, I told them I would dig you up and bring you in."

Edward hovered before her. "And how did they answer that?"

"I did not allow them an answer," she said. "I left."

Dirt rained back down on the ground and across the grave. The wind was laughing. Inside the whirl, her husband held his sides, where his sides would be. Evalene could not help herself; the situation was funny said aloud, and Edward's laughter was always contagious. "You would, too, my Bean," the wind giggled. "You would."

The whirl settled down to a hovering twirl, as they finished their laughing fit. It blew a bit against her face again, and asked, "Do you remember your reply when I wrote you about this claim?"

Evalene frowned. "'You fool man,'" she replied stiffly, quoting her letter. It was a letter she had thought about many times over the years. Edward had, during a brief leave, filed this claim, and, his head hazy from drink, asked for the farthest surveyed area in the land. He sent her the claim before returning to the lines, and she had replied, sent to the field by horse courier.

Edward was gone through by bayonet by the same afternoon.

"Do not be angry with me, Bean," the wind pleaded. "It was not my intention."

She stood up, shaking dirt from her skirts. "I am not proud this was the last I said to you."

"You have said plenty since," the wind replied.

"To a body," she said. "To a ghost. To the wind."

"You do not have anything to worry about, Bean," the wind said. Edward played about her skirts, blowing off the last of the dirt, twirling them about.

"Oh, Edward," she sighed, as the cold rose up to her soft middle flesh. "You fool man."

* * *

Because Paulo and I filed as a family, the claim totaled 320 acres, like the centuries-old Homestead Act this act was modeled after. In school, we learned the first act passed for many of the same reasons as this one: to encourage expansion to the west, although now it had little to do with manifest destiny and everything to do with luring healthy people back across the country, to redistribute overfull population out of the cities that still stood.

With Paulo, I was a better person. When I met him, it was a relief. He had a big personality and a bigger heart, and it was more than enough for both of us.

It was not that he dominated or silenced me, it was just that he was better at being both of us than I was at being myself. He knew just what I wanted, sometimes before I knew.

At the end, I tried to do that for him.

The fever—inevitable, I suppose, although we'd always played against the odds, and were going to cash in, moving far from the fevers out to the wilderness—confined him to our room. But he pretended he was going to recover, and I pretended with him. I completed the industry and vocation coursework, reading lessons to him even as the virus ate him from the inside out. I held him down through the seizures. His hand was always in mine. I sponged him down, spoon-fed him, changed the sheets and then his diapers, and when he died, I closed his eyes.

I tried to stay that person. It was selfish. I came here because Paulo had made the decision we would come here. That was why I placed our data and my tissue samples in cold storage, and traded in my social services card and Paulo's benefits chip for a vial of his remains, a cart full of supplies, a dirty cabin, deer, and talking wind.

Each side of the claim was just under a mile. I walked three quarters of the way before I sat down, sore again, this time from slipping three times on thick undergrowth and falsely solid-looking logs rotten through. Although I was in fine shape, and trained vigorously before ever leaving, it wasn't enough.

Nothing was enough.

I don't know what I thought would happen when I got here. Without Paulo, I didn't commit as much as get swept.

After he died, I collected some of his ashes in the vial. I wove my way home to our room that day, through the teeming streets, I heard Paulo talking of wide open spaces and air clean and heavy with water. My hand around the vial, my eyes changed the skyline to tree lines, and I patted stray dogs and cats like they were our children. I made a promise that day, but acted like it was a vow.

I was drunk on Paulo's stories as a way to keep him with me: hoping the landscape would carry me, a place like Paulo.

People asked me about my plans before I left, and I gave answers, sometimes the same, sometimes different: "Timber," I'd say, or "Fishing," "Trapping," and even occasionally, "Crops."

Maybe that's what that deer saw on my way in. I pictured the deer's eyes, his brown face, and found I could call it up more clearly now than Paulo's. I pulled out the vial as if it would help me remember.

The vial was the same volume as a shot glass. I was overcome by the preciousness of its contents, and now it seemed foolish to dump it out here, let the few flakes of my husband get swallowed into this dark, cold place, never to be found again.

It would tie me here. This claim. That cabin. My home.

I couldn't do it. I slipped the vial back into my pocket. I decided right then to give up and go back. To a tiny bunk in a teeming city. My home.

It wasn't unheard of. I'd repack the cart and ride it back. It would take a few months to reinstate my social card, but I could live off my wits, selling off the supplies on the black market. It was a crime, but not one that would ever be prosecuted, given a number that couldn't come up in my lifetime.

I smiled then, broadly, some because I was relieved, and some to relieve the immediate wave of guilt that swept on me like nausea. I could live with guilt and nausea, I thought, and enjoyed the walk back to the cabin.

It was beautiful country, but cold and wicked somehow, and I wouldn't be sorry to leave it, although I was sorry to fail Paulo. But without him, how could I manage? Would he have expected this of me, knowing me like he did?

Energized, I picked a perfect pinecone off my path to keep as a souvenir. I'd look at it, sitting on a shelf next to the vial of ashes, and over time, this would all fade to a vaguely pleasant memory, like a vacation or a dream.

Wisps of smoke still curled up from the cabin's chimney, testament to my close attention in wildcraft class. I was filled with pride, like any good student, but I was entirely ready to relegate all this to the back of my mind, trivia I knew, things to pull out when cocktail parties grew quiet.

Like someone with a new haircut, I couldn't immediately spot what was different about the cabin. When I did, I stumbled backwards like I'd been pushed.

The cart was gone.

* * *

That one soft inch of fat around her middle was the only thing left of the old Evalene, and the one thing that would not change. It was from being a woman, birthing Thom and Mary, and even as the rest of her grew tight and strong, from cutting, raking, rolling and tying, even as her stance grew wide and solid, that inch of softness reminded her of who she had been.

It jiggled a bit and she jumped up and down at the hay baler to get all her weight onto the compression lever.

She wiped her face, then re-tied the kerchief around her head. When she imagined herself, it was not as she had been: a soft girl, a teenager embroidering to pass the time, a princess bride in thirty pounds of crinoline. Like seeing Edward as the dashing soldier he became at the end, she saw herself as she was now. Disheveled and a little sweaty, but hard headed and taut bodied, all except around her abdomen, which would never disappear.

Next year, they would have enough to hire someone on full time. If they were willing, there was even room for them to build themselves a cabin. Maybe, Evalene thought, she would find someone who'd be willing to teach school. They could build a little schoolhouse; she was willing to donate a bit of edge land for that.

And horses. They would need more than the two they had. The two could each carry two bales of hay, and that was workable making several trips to the bend of the river deep enough to launch the canoe she paddled to deliver the hay. But more horses meant a cart, and a cart could carry more hay— inland, even—and more than two horses needed some sort of stable. It was crowded enough on the coldest nights when she, to the children's delight, led the horses into the cabin.

She let off the lever, and breathed out.

That was when she noticed Jonathan Bonner.

Bonner was strikingly tall, like Edward, but the resemblances ended there. Bonner was built more like a bear than a man, with a round, solid middle and arms and legs nearly too short to support him.

He was strong as a bear, too, and that was why Evalene hired him the first year. He could pull up small trees to the root, and heft logs over his shoulder like a parasol.

Now she knew he was mean as one too. She put her hands on her hips and glared at him, waiting for his business.

Bonner took his hat off, and held it in his hand. "I reckon I am the last person you would hope to come visiting today," he said.

Evalene wiped her hands on her skirt. She had an irrational desire to light one of Edward's cigarettes. Maybe she was growing a taste for them, after all. "I know the land office did not send you."

Bonner looked over her shoulder at the just-baled hay. For a moment, a look passed over his face like he wanted to tear into the pile and eat it up himself. Then it was gone, and he looked back down at her. "No," he said. "But I have come to talk sense about this land."

"Unless that sense is that you have found yours, and you are ending the inquiry, then I have no time for you, Mr. Bonner."

Bonner smiled at that, mouthful of even, sharp little teeth. "No, Mrs. Freeman. I have not called off the inquiry. But you will listen to me."

"Get off my land," Evalene said. Bonner continued to smile, so she added, "Get the hell off my land."

Bonner whistled at that. "You see now, Mrs. Freeman? This is what I am talking about. This isn't a place fit for a lady of your countenance."

That was it. Evalene turned to the back of the barn. She had Edward's gun readied for this. It was one of the three things that came after he died: his body, his wedding ring, and his rosewood and pearl Remington 1858. She's practiced a bit with it, and while she was hardly the best shot, it would be as difficult to miss Jonathan Bonner as the side of the cabin.

But Bonner grabbed her. He was fast, held her around the waist. She squirmed, but he held tight, squeezing her a bit, as that smile grew wider across his face. She was close enough to him to smell his breath, surprisingly sweet, like maple sap, and she could see the fine red spider webs on the whites of his eyes.

He worked his fingers on her fleshy middle. "Where is your corset, woman?" he asked.

Evalene struggled more, but she was like a fish in Thom's net. She didn't answer, and closed her eyes. Whatever was hoping to happen, she did not want to watch it.

But Bonner simply kneaded her back for another second, then shoved her away. "Again," he said. "This proves this is no place for a lady. A proper lady. And her children."

At the word children, Evalene opened her eyes. She listened; she couldn't hear anything except the birds. That did not necessarily mean trouble; Thom and Mary were sensible, well-behaved children.

"This is a wild place," Bonner continued. "Where fine ladies curse and come unbound." Then he leaned back towards her. "And innocent children get called home to the Lord."

At that, Evalene screamed. She screamed for Thom and Mary, and she screamed for Edward.

Bonner started to waddle off, laughing to himself. A wind picked up, picking up dirt and small rocks, but Bonner stepped through the whirl like it was nothing. Edward tried to get at Bonner's horse instead, but Bonner caught and held the reins, and with the grace of having done something a million times before, mounted the mare, even as she whinnied and reared.

"Edward!" Evalene yelled again, but Bonner held in the saddle.

Edward did his best. He blew wind, but it was no use.

"Scaring horses, calling out to ghosts," Jonathan Bonner yelled down to Evalene. "Cussing like a pirate seaman, no undergarments and your children running wild. I think you will see, Mrs. Freeland, that the GLO will agree with me." His mare reared again, but he was set in and rode her down. "This land is not meant for a woman."

Then, Bonner rode away. He was chased by Edward, but didn't know it.

"You fool, fool man," Evalene cried.

* * *

Everything else was as I left it. The fire was nearly out, but the gravel lining kept the cabin warm. I walked inside and outside repeatedly, as if the cart could be hidden somewhere.

I could see on the GPS that it was already nearly five miles away.

I couldn't run that far or that fast, not on the undergrowth or through the trees, compact as a wall in some places.

Did a neighbor send it back? No one was due on the adjoining claims for months. The deer? Ridiculous. It was a malfunction, or there was a timer I didn't know about; it had to be something I overlooked. It had to be.

I sat down on the ground where the cart had been. I didn't cry or yell; I just stared, and then shivered. Wind whipped around my shoulders, and at first I thought I could just sit there and freeze to death, but I couldn't commit to that either. I gave up after I just grew cold and kept living. I went inside, fired up the radio and filed a report.

The cheerful AI took my information, and indicated the cart was returning to the warehouse facility in Denver. I'd be credited, and my next shipment would arrive in six months. I asked if the cart could be redirected back to me, but the AI couldn't process that: the cart was emptied, I was radioing from my claim, if I was injured then I should look to the first aid and medical procedures section of my manual. I hung up in the middle of its monologue—with no satisfaction, knowing that the AI wouldn't register that as anything but the end of a routine transmission.

Six months.

I was stuck here for six months. I could hike back out to the drop off, carrying basics on my back. But no one would be there until the first of my neighbors. And it would leave me with nothing to sell until my services card was reinstated. Nothing to sell except myself, that is, and, in that case, I might as well freeze to death, let myself die.

Stay or go? Live or die? The questions raced through my head until I finally started asking them aloud. I asked the cabin walls, I asked the floor, then I went outside and asked the trees. I asked a squirrel, a wren, a shadow of an elk.

And when the wind started up again, I asked it. I screamed it, and the bodies of trees absorbed it and turned it to a whisper.

Then the wind coalesced and spun, like it had the night before, a twist of air six feet tall. In the light, though, it was apparent it was no devil; it was a man. I could just about make him out inside the spiral, like seeing a shape in a cumulus cloud, only it didn't drift, stretch, or change into something else. He shifted in and out of focus as I backed away.

A breeze blew by me. "Wait," it whispered. "It will be alright."

"Who are you?" I asked it, like it'd asked me. "How do you know?"

The man moved forward, sending out another gust. "My name," he said, "is Captain Edward Thomas Freeman."

He'd been a handsome man, tall and thin, but elegant. His clothes were strange to me, old-fashioned. "I have watched you and listened." He progressed forward again, and continued. "You are here alone."

"Yes," I answered. "I am."

A finger of air branched out by my ear. "Where is your husband? Your family?"

"My husband is in my pocket." I pulled out and held up the vial.

Captain Freeman's face flashed confusion, then sank back to blurry.

"He died," I explained. I thought of my tissue samples flash frozen in City Hall. "No children."

The captain looked sad for me, for a second. Like the deer, he thought now he knew something about me, like that was why I was out here, yelling at the trees and the sky and the ground, carpeted with moss and pine needles.

"Why are you here, then?" he asked.

"Coming here was my husband's idea. Get out of the city, start over, get back to nature," I said. "He thought the city would kill us."

I didn't see the captain move forward, but then he was right next to me. The air around him was freezing cold, and I breathed out vapor, like it was winter.

"This had been my notion, as well," he said. "This land was my dream."

"I am waking up from the dream," I said. "I want to go home." I put the vial back in my pocket and wrapped my arms around myself.

"Perchance, do you have any tobacco?" Captain Freeman asked. "I had a habit, and it has been many years." His face jerked a little inside the wind, like a bad connection. "You are the first to answer."

I had the packs of cigarettes issued with the supplies. "I do, actually," I answered.

"Would you be as kind as to get one?" he asked. "My appreciation would be great."

"You can smoke?"

"No," he said. "But perhaps you could light it, and blow smoke to me?"

I'd never smoked, and Captain Freeman could see it on my face. "My wife did not care for tobacco either, but she would humor me. She developed a taste eventually, though."

"You lived here with your wife?"

"I never lived here," he said. "I, I died. Like your husband. But my wife and my children came." He dispersed for a second into mist, then tightened back into view. "My wife had me sent and buried here. As you have taken your husband with you." He paused, "But I failed her. I could not help her. I could not help my children."

"What happened to your wife? To your children?" I asked. I looked at the man inside the wind.

"I can help you," he said.

"You are wind," I answered.

"You will not fail."

"What happened to your family?" I asked again.

"I have grown stronger since then," he said. "Watch." Then he blew at a young conifer. The branches bent some, and plucked off loose needles. Then he looked at me, but didn't see what he wanted. "I can help you," he repeated. "I am stronger. My wind blew away your vessel."

"You trapped me here," I whispered, then stated, then yelled. I clawed at the man, but my hands went right through. I tore and punched and slashed at him until I wanted to sink down with exhaustion.

But the captain held me up with an icy cold wind. "You will not fail."

Then he placed his arms around me. I was inside the wind. "You fool," I sobbed, though I wasn't sure I meant him or me.

"There now, Bean," he whispered to my ear, close, like a lover. "We will not fail. We are proving up."

About the Authors

Jordan Taylor

Jordan Taylor's short fiction has appeared in magazines including Uncanny and Beneath Ceaseless Skies, and was nominated for a World Fantasy Award. Though she's lived in cities across the US, she's finally settled in North Carolina in a little cottage full of books. You can follow her online at jordantaylorwrites.com, or on Twitter @JordanRTaylor13.

Laura Hennessey DeSena

Laura Hennessey DeSena teaches AP English Literature, Creative Writing, and Doppelgangers, Dreams, & Madness: The Gothic Landscape. For nearly two decades, she taught composition and research writing at NYU's School of Continuing and Professional Studies. Her performance pieces, "Eve Speaks to Cain," "Eden Within Us," and her play, "The Men's Club," have been staged in theatres in NYC and in New Jersey. Her articles of literary criticism are included in Contemporary Women Artists (St. Martin's Press, 1999). She is the author of Preventing Plagiarism: Tips and Techniques published by the National Council of Teachers of English (2007). She was invited to be an advisor in the revision of Turabian's College Student Writing published by University of Chicago Press (2010) and she served as an expert for the Online Writing Institute Conference on College Composition and Communication (CCCC).

Raised on her grandmother's stories from the turn of the last century about a coal mining town, Summit Hill, Pennsylvania, she threads together their remnants: the men and women of this town, their superstitions, and their everyday heroic lives still enliven her dreams.

LH Moore

LH Moore's stories, poetry and essays have appeared in numerous anthologies and publications such as FIYAH, Apex and Fireside. A historian who loves playing video games and classical guitar, you can find her online at lhmoorecreative.com, tweeting @ElleHM or on IG: @lh_moore.

Stephen K Pettersson

Stephen Karl Pettersson is a Swedish author of LGBTQ+ inclusive fiction — writing primarily in fantasy and magical realism. While "The Song of the Iron Woods" is Stephen's first published work, he has written and created stories for as long as he can remember. His writing started with handmade comic books about incredibly spiky swamp monsters, and has since evolved (or devolved, depending on your perspective) to focus on the more human element of fantasy. But then again: it wouldn't be fantasy without the odd mythical creature, spell or prophecy.

Being a gay writer has informed Stephen of the absolute need for more diversity and representation in fiction. As a result, his stories often include queer themes and/or characters in the hopes that his readers will see a little piece of themselves in his work — a piece so often overlooked in short fiction.

Stephen currently lives in the former mining town of Falun with his mother Karin and his two pets: Zimba the cat, and Gizmo the dog. When he's not writing, you might find him with good friends in passionate discussions about philosophy and politics, or in a gaming chair making a fool out of himself in Valorant or The Witcher 3.

Henry Herz

Henry Herz's speculative fiction short stories include Out, Damned Virus (Daily Science Fiction), Bar Mitzvah on Planet Latke (Albert Whitman & Co.), The Crowe Family (Castle of Horror V, Castle Bridge Media), Demon Hunter Vashti (The Jewish Book of Horror, Denver Horror Collective), Alien with a Bad Attitude (Strangely Funny VIII, Mystery and Horror LLP), The Case of the Murderous Alien (Spirit Machine, Air and Nothingness Press), Maria & Maslow (Highlights for Children), A Proper Party (Ladybug Magazine). He's written ten picture books, including the critically acclaimed I Am Smoke. *Henry's edited three anthologies, including* The Hitherto Secret Experiments of Marie Curie *(Blackstone Publishing) and* Coming of Age *(Albert Whitman & Co.). Find him at www.henryherz.com.*

Jane Nightshade

A native Californian, Jane Nightshade is a former corporate writer turned literary horror, sci-fi, speculative, and crime writer. Her non-fiction writing about horror/crime film and television has appeared online at Horrornews.net, Horrified Magazine (https://www.horrifiedmagazine.co.uk/), Ghouls Magazine (https://www.ghoulsmagazine.com/), and Mandatory Midnight (davidpaulharris.com). Her fiction has appeared in several anthologies and has been dramatized by NoSleep Podcast and Octoberpod. She is the author of The Drowning Game, A Novella of the Supernatural, *available in digital form on Amazon.*

Colleen Ennen

Colleen Ennen is a writer, teacher, project manager, and professional "nightmare woman" living and working and reading and writing in Minneapolis. She received her MFA in Writing from Sarah Lawrence College in 2019, writes unsettling and uncanny fiction (and sometimes creative nonfiction), and is at work on her first novel. In the meantime, her writing has appeared in The Lit Pub, LUMINA, Moon-Birds, and Breadcrumbs Magazine. In her spare time she enjoys hiking, baking, witching, accidentally killing all her plants, and watching every procedural and mystery show known to humankind. Find her being occasionally funny on Twitter at @abitunsettling.

Caren Gussoff Sumption

Caren Gussoff Sumption is a SF writer of mixed Romany ancestry, living near Seattle, WA. The author of 5 books and more than 100 short stories, Caren Gussoff Sumption's been awarded a Hedgebrook Elizabeth George Award, the Speculative Literature Foundation's Gulliver Grant, a stint as the Seattle Post-Intelligencer's Geek of the Week, and honors from the European Commission on Science and Society.

She received her MFA from the School of the Art Institute of Chicago, and in 2008, was the Carl Brandon Society's Octavia E. Butler Scholar at Clarion West. Her latest work is forthcoming from Vernacular Books in 2022, and a full list of her publications can be found at www.spitkitten.com.

Source Acknowledgements

"La Orpheline", Jordan Taylor, First Published in: *Beneath Ceaseless Skies, Issue #269*, Firkin Press, 2019.

"With These Hands", LH Moore, First Published in: *FIYAH Literary Magazine of Black Speculative Fiction, Issue #5*, NSS Media, 2018.

"Proving Up", Caren Gussoff Sumption, First Published in: *Shades of Blue and Gray: Ghosts of the Civil War*, Prime Books, 2013.